"Erynn, ge[...]"

Noah's shoulde[...] the gunshot. Pain exploded in her wrist, w[...] fallen on. Noah was shielding her with his body.

Willing to die so she wouldn't have to. Just like her dad.

A sob choked Erynn's throat, but she was powerless to move. "Where is he?"

"On top of one of the buildings."

Another shot, this one close enough that the broken sidewalk sprayed pieces of concrete in her direction, hitting her on the arm.

"We've got to move. You can't get shot because of me." He just couldn't.

"We need to run. See the bushes to the right?" They'd known each other long enough, Erynn guessed, that their minds were in sync enough that they moved as one toward cover.

He'd almost gotten killed. Because of her. Grief pressed in, suffocated her with its weight.

To think she'd been close to hoping maybe she and Noah could talk about what they'd avoided discussing or confronting about their feelings for so many years.

She couldn't now.

Couldn't ever.

Sarah Varland lives in Alaska with her husband, John, their two boys and their dogs. Her passion for books comes from her mom; her love for suspense comes from her dad, who has spent a career in law enforcement. When she's not writing, she's often found dog mushing, hiking, reading, kayaking, drinking coffee or enjoying other Alaskan adventures with her family.

Books by Sarah Varland

Love Inspired Suspense

Treasure Point Secrets
Tundra Threat
Cold Case Witness
Silent Night Shadows
Perilous Homecoming
Mountain Refuge
Alaskan Hideout
Alaskan Ambush
Alaskan Christmas Cold Case

Visit the Author Profile page at Harlequin.com.

ALASKAN CHRISTMAS COLD CASE

SARAH VARLAND

⟨H⟩ HARLEQUIN® LOVE INSPIRED® SUSPENSE

Recycling programs
for this product may
not exist in your area.

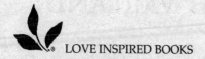

® LOVE INSPIRED BOOKS

ISBN-13: 978-1-335-23242-7

Alaskan Christmas Cold Case

Copyright © 2019 by Sarah Varland

www.Harlequin.com

Printed in U.S.A.

There is no fear in love;
but perfect love casteth out fear: because fear
hath torment. He that feareth is not made perfect in love.
−1 John 4:18

To my family. I'm so thankful for all of you.

ONE

Someone had been watching her. All morning, maybe even for the last few days. Goose bumps would run down Erynn Cooper's arms at the oddest time. In the grocery store, while she was walking from her truck in the parking lot to the trooper building in the mornings...

And she was afraid she knew who. He—or she—had been responsible for five deaths already, six counting her father's.

She'd always known he would come for her.

Erynn closed the door behind her, debated locking it, but knew that wasn't why she was in town. She was not running; she was simply trying to live her life, fill her dad's shoes in any way she could by bringing criminals to justice, helping people feel safe. And keep her ears out for any leads on the cold case that had led to her dad's death.

Most days she felt like she could barely fill half of one of Mack Cooper's shoes. Why had he been the one to die so young?

And what would her life have been like if he hadn't? She wouldn't have become a trooper, Erynn didn't think, but what would she have been?

She'd never had the chance to consider it, not really.

She sat at her desk, shoved aside the little Christmas tree her partner had apparently added while she'd been home sleeping, and poured herself a cup of coffee. She had already told him she wasn't big on Christmas decorations. Apparently he didn't care. Every day this week it had been something new. First twinkling lights, then snowman stickers on the windows. Now the tree. Erynn shook her head and took a sip of coffee, startling as her phone chimed the arrival of a text message.

Noah.

You weren't at the diner last night. Everything okay?

Almost every Saturday night the two of them, along with some friends, played board games at the diner while drinking bad coffee and talking about their weeks. She hadn't wanted to go last night since yesterday had been odd and she'd felt out of place all day, like something was wrong.

It hadn't been until this morning that she'd pinpointed the feeling: she was prey and someone was hunting her, or at the very least watching her. But she hadn't wanted to face Noah when she hadn't felt her best. Despite her efforts, the man knew her too well. And she didn't want him getting any closer to her, prying into her life any more.

It would only make things more dangerous for both of them. Her life. His career.

She took a deep breath then a sip of coffee. She had a job to do, and she needed to focus and do it.

Hours passed uneventfully. Erynn glanced at her watch. Less than an hour until she was done for the day.

Then what? Go home and hide in her apartment again? Or see if she could find who was watching her? She had her training on her side, wouldn't be caught off guard.

Then again, her dad had probably thought the same. Pain stabbed her heart and she shook her head. If only this feeling would shake off so easily.

The door creaked open.

In stepped her past in the form of Janie Davis. Erynn felt her jaw tense and a headache start at the corners of her temples. She blinked, but Janie was still standing there. Back from the dead, or so it appeared. And, with her appearance, the heaviness that had crowded Erynn's high school years, like clouds hanging low over the ocean on a stormy day, also returned.

She'd known Janie from their time in foster care years ago. Erynn couldn't breathe, couldn't move. Seeing her past find her here, in her office, at work, would have shaken her enough…but Janie Davis had died three years ago, her body having been found near Moose Haven, on a glacier. Erynn had been one of the officers who had worked the case, along with Noah Dawson and the rest of the Moose Haven Police Department. Except clearly she hadn't died. Because here she was in the Moose Haven Trooper Station.

Would she ever escape her past?

"What are you doing here?" Erynn shook her head, stood and moved to the windows, pulled the blinds and then looked back at her unexpected visitor. "Never mind. Don't answer yet. I need another set of ears here." She hated to do it; it went against every ounce of energy she'd spent this week, keeping him at a distance. But Noah's was the best law enforcement mind for miles around, besides hers. And his team was good, too. She trusted them and she needed help, preferably from another agency, because if she was right about why Janie was there…this was about to blow up in their faces and they'd all need to work together.

She slid her cell phone from her pocket, deciding texting was the fastest way to get Noah's attention.

S.O.S. I need you at the Trooper station.

He took only seconds to text back.

You're safe?

Erynn glanced up at the blonde, whose gaze hadn't left her.

Not sure.

He should be there within minutes. The two law enforcement offices were separated by two blocks and Erynn was all too aware that when it came to Noah and her… Well, it was complicated. Not something she had space in her life for. But she knew he wouldn't let anything happen to her if he could help it.

"I can't believe you aren't happy to see me." Janie's voice was much the same as it had been when they were kids living in the same group home, but more grown-up now, a little husky.

"You've been missing. We thought you were dead. Found a body and it matched your description…"

"I'm not dead. And I wasn't missing. I was hiding. There's a difference."

Someone knocked on the door.

"Would have been nice if you'd clarified that with law enforcement." Erynn moved to the door, slid one of the blind slats wider with her fingers to confirm it was Noah, then let him in. They had butted heads more times than she could count in the years she'd been working Moose Haven and he'd been the police chief. But she had his back, knew he had hers.

Today they needed to work together more than they ever had.

Because if the weighty sense of foreboding that sat on Erynn's shoulders right now had any bearing on reality… they were all in trouble.

And she and Janie were in danger.

"Is this…?" Noah trailed off, glancing at Janie then at Erynn. She knew he'd seen the missing person's posters and the photos they'd passed around during the search. He also knew about the eventual discovery of the remains they'd assumed were hers in a crevasse in Harding Ice-field, the ice field that connected Moose Haven's Raven Glacier to Seward's more well-known Exit Glacier.

But he hadn't known Janie in person the way Erynn had. And, maybe worse, he hadn't known about Erynn's relationship to her, either. She hadn't known how to admit that the case had edged toward personal for her, had danced toward the line of her possibly having to not be on the case.

Because it hadn't seemed necessary.

Because they'd needed her.

Because she'd cared too much about it to let it out of her hands.

In all the years he'd known Erynn, Noah had never seen her like this. She was the one in control of situations, sure of herself and bossy to a fault. The woman in front of him right now? He didn't know what could have made her so upset.

However, the fact that someone they'd both thought was dead was standing in the trooper station? It wasn't a good sign. Scratch that—it had been *Noah* who had thought they should stop looking at the case, and the rest of the Moose Haven Police Department and the troopers had agreed with him. The case had gone cold; everything had pointed to the possibility it could have been an accident. Erynn's assertions that they should look more closely at the situation had been ignored.

He was wishing he'd listened to her now.

"This is Janie Davis." Erynn's voice was steady but not as steely as usual. Noah waited, not wanting to step into what was technically her case at the moment since Janie had come to her. But Erynn just stood there. Staring. Her face had paled and he watched as she swallowed hard.

There would be time for her to argue with him about this later, but for now he was going to handle things.

"Janie, I'm Noah Dawson, the Moose Haven Police Chief. Can we sit down? We have some questions for you, as you might have assumed, and I'm hoping your presence here means you intend to answer them."

She shook her head. "I want to talk to Erynn."

Erynn. Why did she use her first name? Most people would have said "Trooper Cooper."

Noah looked at his friend. At the woman who had been tying his insides in knots for years—both professionally and personally, whether she knew it or not.

"Since Chief Dawson and I work together on cases often, he needs to be here, too." Erynn spoke up. "Let's go into my office." She looked at Noah, met his eyes, but he couldn't tell what, if anything, she was trying to convey.

He followed her down the short hallway, into her office, mentally pulling up everything he'd known about the case. They had initially referred to the woman in the glacier crevasse outside Seward as "The Ice Maiden" before linking that case to the disappearance of a woman in Anchorage named Janie Davis. She had matched the description—even though they'd never been able to recover the body. It had been deemed too dangerous, something that was not rare in the Alaskan backcountry.

Maybe he should have pushed for that, told Erynn's superiors who had flown out that leaving a body left questions unanswered and was unacceptable. People went missing in Alaska, died in accidents all the time. With no solid evidence that the Ice Maiden had been murdered, they'd been forced—or so Noah had felt, anyway—to draw the conclusion that the death had been accidental.

He was questioning that now.

Realistically, Noah wasn't sure what he could have done, pushing to keep a case open that the troopers had thought was closed. The working relationship between the Moose Haven Police Department and the state troopers could have been compromised.

Noah had regrets but didn't know if he'd change anything, even if he could go back. They'd done the best they could.

Except he wished he had some power to take away the haunted look in Erynn's eyes. Who was this woman to her? She'd known her before. He was almost sure of that now.

But how did Janie fit?

"We could arrest you for obstruction of justice, are you aware of that?" Erynn took the lead and did it well. She had been shaken earlier but she'd recovered. Noah should have known she would have. She'd taken a seat behind her desk and sat there now, leaned back, arms crossed. He felt his own shoulders relax. She could handle this.

"Wouldn't just be me being arrested." Janie met Erynn's eyes.

Noah didn't like what he saw there.

Erynn said nothing.

Noah tried to meet her eyes. Decided to step in, maybe rile up Janie enough so Erynn could get hold of herself again.

"What are you implying, Miss Davis?"

"I think you both know."

"Trooper Cooper is an outstanding officer and has worked too hard on every case she's ever had. She takes her job seriously and I won't listen to you saying otherwise. Are you ready to leave now? Because I can show you out the door."

A sideways glance told him Erynn didn't look relieved. If anything, she'd paled even more. She shook her head. "You can't let her leave."

He knew that already. Didn't have to like it, but he knew it. If Janie had been hiding and her disappearance from society had something to do with the Ice Maiden's body...then it likely wasn't a typical case of someone disappearing in the backcountry. The troopers and police forces would need to reopen the case, see if it could have been a homicide. Which meant that Janie was an important witness in a case that had gone cold years ago. However, what he didn't know was why she showed so much familiarity with Erynn.

Noah had known Erynn for five years. Trusted her more than he did anyone else, except maybe his brother and Clay, his second-in-command at the PD. Between them, though, it was a tie. And Noah didn't give his trust easily. It just wasn't in his nature.

He looked at Erynn. Waited. But she didn't meet his eyes. Wouldn't.

He'd have to handle this himself. Talk to Erynn later.

"Let's start with right now and work backward. You aren't dead."

"That's correct."

"Are you aware that you've been declared so?"

The body they'd found in the crevasse had matched Janie Davis's description. The woman had gone missing at the same time. They'd interviewed witnesses, tracked her movements up until she'd come to Seward, a town near Moose Haven, and disappeared.

It hadn't been shoddy police work that had made the case go cold. Or that had led them to believe the death could have been accidental. Someone had known what they were doing, had intended for them to think Janie Davis was dead.

But she wasn't.

So who *was* she?

"I was aware," Janie was saying, her facial expression still so cocky that it made Noah immediately suspicious. He wasn't willing to discount the possibility that she was involved in a way that did make her a criminal.

"So you've come to turn yourself in."

"It's not like that."

"No?" Noah asked.

"I've been hiding to protect myself."

Yeah, because he'd never heard that before. "For three years." It was a statement, not a question.

"You wouldn't understand." Janie looked at Erynn.

Erynn met *her* gaze.

And not his? How well did she know this person? They didn't strike him as friends. Someone from far back in her past?

"Why did you come here?" Noah asked.

"Because I'm tired of knowing that he's still out there, that he could get away with more crimes. I'm tired of looking over my shoulder, of wondering if I'm going to cost anyone else their life."

"Are you saying the woman in the glacier is dead because of you?" Noah spoke up again, glanced at Erynn, who had stayed quiet. She'd turned into an observer.

Janie shook her head. "No. But I may end up dead because of her. And I'm worried that if I do…Erynn will end up dead because of me. I needed to come here, needed to make sure she had all the information so she could find him, make him stop."

"No one's going to let you be killed," Noah said.

"It's not a promise you can make, I'm afraid."

"Why don't you tell us what you came to say and then let us do our best?"

He watched the woman consider. Waited.

And wondered why someone would be after Erynn.

TWO

If she could go back, if she could undo the last near decade of silence, Erynn would do it. But she'd always believed life should be lived looking forward, not backward.

Too bad that's not how you've been living.

She listened to Noah question Janie, listened to Janie's explanations, while she ran through the list of possible suspects in her mind, knowing her chances of landing on one that stuck weren't good since the Anchorage Police Department and the State Troopers had tried back then.

Come up empty.

And then her father had been killed. An Anchorage police officer, he'd been investigating the Foster Kid Murders...the killings they'd thought had claimed the lives of three other victims at the time. Five total. Erynn had worried the murderer had claimed Janie's life, as well.

Erynn blinked, tried to focus on the present and the conversation, reminded herself that she wasn't to blame for her father's death. Mack Cooper had been investigating the case even before he'd adopted her, which was why the Anchorage Police Department hadn't considered his involvement a conflict of interest. He'd adopted her later, and had told her that were it not for the serial killer case, he and his wife might never have looked into adopting from foster care. They'd wanted her, they'd both emphasized that over and over, and in her heart, Erynn knew that her dad wouldn't have gone back and changed a thing. Still, guilt stabbed deep. He had given his life to protect her, for those like her. It packed a punch, even this many years later.

And Erynn missed him.

She listened to their voices, tried to distract herself from the flood of emotions threatening to wash over her. They'd gone quiet after Noah had asked Janie what she'd come to tell them. Waited as Janie considered whether she was ready to.

"I was living in Kenai three years ago when I got a message from a friend in Anchorage. Michelle Holt."

Erynn knew who she meant. She'd known Michelle even less than she'd known Janie, but she remembered the two of them being close back in high school.

She glanced at Noah, feeling for once that his eyes weren't on her. He had been looking at her strangely since he'd come in; she guessed she didn't blame him. She was far from her usual self today. Right now, though, his gaze was on Janie and he was waiting for her to continue, not asking anything.

A smart move. She'd have done the same in his shoes. He was handling this well. She should have known he would.

Well, up until he found out the full truth about Erynn. No one knew how he'd handle that.

"The message said she was in danger. She'd been working in Seward for the summer and I knew she needed my help. I went to Seward, found her before he did."

"He?"

"I'm getting there. Please don't interrupt.

"I managed to find her first and we talked. She told me he was after her, that he'd left her messages, talked about finding the rest of the kids from his list—though we were adults by that time—and finishing what he'd started."

Erynn could have thrown up. Probably would have if there had been a trash can within reach. Instead she took a deep breath and willed her stomach and the rest of her to hold it together. She'd known what it probably meant when Janie had walked in. But she hadn't been sure.

Turned out knowing in this case was much, *much* worse than not knowing.

"What list?" Noah asked. Erynn felt every muscle tense, tried to do one of the breathing exercises she'd learned years back.

Erynn felt Janie's eyes on her. Refused to meet her look as Janie continued, "Someone was killing foster kids."

"When?"

"Years ago," Janie continued. "Then he stopped. Went silent and I guess we let our guard down. That's when he came after me and Michelle. I never heard from her, after she warned me. I suspect she's the one the media referred to as the Ice Maiden. The one you thought was me."

Noah was nodding, a quick glance at him confirmed. Erynn looked away before he could see her staring.

Janie continued. "I told her we should call the police, but she reminded me that it would just put them in danger. At least one officer was killed investigating the case when it was making news and hot. I'm not sure if the police ever said his death was related, but those of us the Foster Kid Killer was after, we knew."

Her dad. Erynn stood. Left the room to be sick. She could not hear Janie's words from where she was in the bathroom. She'd have more questions from Noah to answer. But she'd not be able to help it.

Her forehead was hot and her heartbeat pounded in her ears. Breathe in, breathe out, she reminded herself as she'd had to do in the days after her father's death when it had all seemed like *too much*. She reached for the sink knob, turned on the cold water and splashed her face.

Breathed in. Breathed out. And walked back into the lobby, not sure she was ready to hear anything else. But knowing she couldn't hide forever.

This had proven that.

"What else can you tell me about the killer?"

"He…" Janie trailed off. "There's not much I know, to be honest, just suspicions. Speculations. I always wondered if he'd met us personally. Maybe it always feels personal when someone is after you and your friends. But I wondered."

"Have you seen him? Anything you know, we could use as a solid lead."

"No."

"We'll need to put you in protective custody," Noah was saying even as Janie shook her head.

Erynn had known she would. That's the kind of woman Janie was. Once her mind was made up, there'd be no changing it.

"I'm going back home now. I just thought you should know."

Could they keep her? Charge her with something that would allow them to keep her safe? Even as the thoughts surfaced, Erynn shrugged them off. It was still a free country and if Janie didn't want protection, they didn't need to give it to her.

Noah spoke again. "Then we're officially charging you with obstruction of justice and you can come with me to the Moose Haven jail."

If she'd been able to feel even a smidgen more light-hearted, Erynn would have laughed. The Moose Haven jail was no more than two cells in the back of the police department, Wild West style, that the department had gotten built cheap.

Still, it would work for what they needed, would do the job.

"Are you arresting Erynn, also?"

Erynn looked at Noah, met his eyes. Knew she owed him answers.

"Not at this time."

She needed to talk to him tonight.

"For now, come with me, please."

Noah had left over half an hour ago, had practically growled at her to "stay put." She had, quite literally, and hadn't moved from her desk.

Janie.

Her dad.

This couldn't be happening.

Erynn laid her head in her hands, snapped it up again as she realized all the implications. They had Janie in custody because it was dangerous for her otherwise. What Erynn had realized but not fully felt the weight of until now was that if someone was after her old acquaintance…had killed another one of her former friends, if Janie was right and Michelle was the Ice Maiden…

She wasn't safe, either.

She stood and walked to the window, put a hand on the flimsy mini-blinds as she looked out at the town of Moose Haven. She'd thought the assignment here years ago had worked out well. It was close enough to civilization to suit her—she wasn't a "live in the Alaskan bush" kind of girl, but it was far enough from Anchorage to make her believe she could get away from the demons, both real and imagined, chasing her.

But she hadn't gotten away. Not really. Erynn closed the blinds, moved back to the hallway and headed toward the front to close the other blinds. And lock the door. Noah could call or knock when he got there. She checked her watch. Her shift was over in ten minutes. Trooper Miller, a new transfer fresh out of the academy, should be in to relieve her at any minute.

The door opened just then and Miller walked in. "Whoa, you don't look so good."

The kid had barely met the minimum age requirement for the troopers—at least, that was Erynn's guess. He made her feel light-years old and, at just barely thirty, she didn't appreciate it.

"Not feeling so great, to be honest."

"Go ahead and head out. I've got this."

"I'll wait till it's officially time." Miller was a decent kid so far, and Erynn trusted him, but he wasn't the stickler for protocol that older officers she'd worked with had been. Good for some situations, not that she'd admit that on the record, but bad for others.

Noah still hadn't showed by the time she was ready

to head home. Erynn hesitated half a second at the door then shook her head and went outside. She'd been a State Trooper for years. She'd taken self-defense courses, had a sidearm on her right side concealed under her windbreaker right now.

She wasn't technically in any more danger than she had been for years. She had known she'd never truly be safe.

Not until the Ice Maiden Killer—who, it seemed, was also the Foster Kid Killer—was in custody.

"What are you doing?"

Noah's voice was hard as she came around the corner of the building and almost ran into him.

"I can't stay here all night." Not that she'd sleep at home. Maybe she should stay here, sleep on the office couch, but it would invite too many questions. Her job was one of the only things she had left, was the most important part of her life. She couldn't lose it, too.

"I told you to stay put."

Maybe it was the coldness in his voice. Maybe it was the fact that the day had had more surprises than she could handle on the amount of sleep she was running on currently, but she'd lost all her patience.

"You aren't in charge of me, Noah. I'm an adult and make my own decisions."

"I want to hear more about why she'd say you'd obstructed justice. And why you didn't deny a word of it."

She turned to him, mouth open, but nothing came out. She didn't know what she wanted to say anyway, just couldn't believe he was looking at her that way.

Like she was guilty of something.

Her shoulders fell. At the very least, she could assure him that wasn't the case—though, yes, it would have been better for her to have spoken up three years ago when the Ice Maiden case had come across their desks. She could have told him that she'd worried that Janie's "death" had been the work of the Foster Kid Killer, as Janie dying accidentally when so many people she'd known had been killed had seemed too coincidental to her. But when the other officers had ruled it an accidental death, something far too common in the Alaskan wilderness, she'd hoped it was true. Thought maybe she was paranoid. Hadn't wanted to believe they were all wrong and she was right.

It had been murder.

But she hadn't obstructed justice. She'd just…stayed quiet. Erynn rubbed a hand across her forehead, winced against the throbbing of her building headache. She'd wanted so badly to be free from the fear, that entire chapter of her life, that she'd ignored the coincidence it would have been that a former foster kid she'd known had ended up dead.

She exhaled. "Okay. Where do you want to go?"

"My house."

She nodded. "I'll follow you there."

"No. You can ride with me."

She didn't have the energy to argue.

Noah did not have anything to say on their drive. What was there to say? "Hi, I'm Noah Dawson. Who are you *really*?" He'd known the woman for five years and she'd never once mentioned a connection to a serial killer case in Anchorage, or the fact that her life was ever in danger at all. She'd acted like a Moose Haven native, hanging out at the diner, doing the polar plunge into the bay in January, but she had secrets.

He'd never even imagined that. Maybe that's why it hurt so much.

He turned down the gravel drive to his place, stealing a glance at Erynn as he parked the car.

She was just looking out the window. Silent and more serious than he'd ever seen her. Wasn't she the one always telling him to loosen up? Calm down? She'd been a steadying influence more than once, but now he felt like he didn't even know this woman next to him.

"Erynn?" He finally broke the silence after they'd been sitting for a full minute and she still hadn't moved.

"I'm sorry." She unbuckled, turned to him when he didn't move. "Are you ready?"

Was he? He didn't know. "Just waiting for you."

True in more ways than she knew.

She pushed her door open. He did the same, stood to follow her to his front door, eyes open and scanning—he didn't think she faced danger but better safe than—

Erynn stopped.

Noah did the same. Seeing nothing. "What is it?"

"On your porch. What's that on the table?"

He squinted. The sun was still high in the sky even at this time of evening, due to Alaska's midnight sun, and the rays were in his eyes. He didn't see what had her so riled.

Noah stepped forward. There it was. A piece of paper?

Part of him rebelled against the idea that she could be spooked by pieces of paper. That wasn't the woman he knew. And this was Moose Haven. He'd worked quite a few crimes here, but the town as a whole was still sort of an Alaskan coastal Mayberry. It felt wrong for her to be so on edge here.

Still, before his brother, Tyler, had gotten married,

someone had been after his future wife, Emma. Tyler had been able to reassure Emma that she was safe and Emma had trusted him.

Erynn knew too much to be that easily reassured. A threat could come out of nowhere. And if she was acting like this, there was a reason.

God, help me listen when she's ready to talk. And help me know what to do. He prayed in his head, even as he started toward Erynn. He wasn't going to be able to do this on his own. "Stay with me. We'll go check it out together."

She swallowed hard but offered him a small smile. At least he'd said the right thing this time.

He fought the urge to reach for her hand, settling instead for a hand on her back as he guided her along. Perfectly platonic. Not at all over the firm boundaries of their friendship and history as coworkers.

Again, nothing like his brother had been through. Or his sisters, for that matter. His siblings had found love amid danger, but Noah had long since given up on that for himself.

Because the only woman he was interested in had walls around her heart a mile high and he'd long ago realized that if he wanted to keep her as a friend he needed to respect those restrictions.

"It's a note," he said as they got closer to the table.

She reached for it.

"Don't."

She stopped at the sound of his voice, speared him with a look. "What are we going to do, call the police? We are the police, Noah."

"I am. You're a *trooper*. I believe you've been pretty clear about that a few times." He couldn't resist teasing her. Moose Haven treated its police officers well, but Alaska state troopers were proud of their title, their elite standing in the law enforcement world.

She made a face and, despite the tension in the air, despite the fact that Noah was looking over his shoulder—their shoulders—every few seconds, it felt good to know that whatever else was going on now, they still had a friendship. Or he thought they did.

Erynn reached for the paper, paused and looked at him.

"Same paper."

"As what?"

She shook her head.

"I'm going to need the pieces I'm missing, Erynn, or I can't help."

He watched her face as emotions chased across it. She had never been good at hiding her feelings, except in work circumstances, and then she'd managed.

Erynn said, "It's the same paper the serial killer Janie mentioned left with all of his victims. Thick, cream stationery. The blue ink is nothing special, your general economy pens available at any store. The paper comes from a special company, but they went out of business fifty years ago. Someone's got a stockpile of the stuff and it's impossible to trace."

She paused. His mind spun in circles, trying to think through everything she'd just said.

After a moment Erynn reached forward again, picked up the stationery.

She's mine. You're next. And then it's over.

Noah managed to read the words before she dropped the paper, watched as it fluttered to the table. She was back to looking pale again. He needed to get her inside, to feed her, to hear what was going on so he didn't feel like he was always a couple of steps behind.

Wait. He grabbed up the note. "'She's mine'? He's talking about—"

"Janie." Erynn ran back to the car. "We have to get Janie out of the jail." Noah followed her.

"She's there to keep her safe, Erynn. There are officers in the building. She's fine."

"She's not fine, Noah, trust me."

She'd asked him to trust her once. To keep the Ice Maiden case open, against the advice of every other law enforcement officer involved.

He hadn't done it.

"Let's go."

They backed out of the driveway, note carefully put inside a notebook on the back seat. They would process it for prints or any other trace evidence, though if this guy had been terrorizing and killing people for longer than a decade, Noah held out little hope it would hold anything useful.

"So much I didn't say to her…" Erynn muttered. "I didn't thank her for coming. Didn't tell her I was sorry I didn't figure it out sooner…"

"You figured out more than we did about that case, it seems like. More than anyone else."

Erynn shook her head. "Not really. I had a hunch, that was all, but you can't take a hunch to court. Can't keep a case open for one."

"You can tell her everything you want when we get there."

She just shook her head again. "You don't understand how he works."

"Then tell me, Erynn. Tell me everything."

"I've known him to take people from their beds while they were sleeping, with no one in the house disturbed, all the doors firmly locked when he left. He's gotten people who were under police protection. Got an officer…"

"Janie told me you knew the officer who was killed."

Erynn looked at him like she was asking him a question, asking his eyes, but didn't say anything.

"She'll be okay." He believed it or he wouldn't say it.

"She won't."

They drove on. His phone rang half a mile from Moose Haven.

Janie Davis was dead.

THREE

Erynn could not remember the last time she'd cried, but she knew it had been years, likely connected to this case. But she wanted to now. If only she could make the tears come, relieve the pressure building in her face and forehead…

She'd been too late. Again.

Beside her, Noah's body language was another worry to contend with. The man was past worked up, more so than she'd ever seen him. On most of the cases they'd worked together, Erynn would have taken it upon herself to help him calm down, to bring some perspective.

Today she had nothing to give him. Wasn't sure she had much left to give herself.

Janie was dead.

Erynn couldn't see how she was supposed to escape the same fate. Not when every single person this killer had ever come after was dead. He'd already found Noah's house, realized their connection.

"I wanted to be able to look at you for this conversation, not driving, but I need to know now, Erynn. Who and what are we dealing with? What do you know?"

He had managed to say the last part with no accusation in his voice.

She might be a lot of things, but she'd never hinder progress, especially not in this case. Didn't Noah get that? This was her life, not just her.

Erynn had lost everything that mattered to her before. And thanks to this killer, she'd already come close again.

She didn't want that to happen. Didn't want to die. She drew in a shaky breath. "It's faster if you search for some of the details online—they're all out there. Someone handed the press quite the lovely story." Her first brush with how newspapers could destroy an investigation. Let one detail slip at the wrong time, let the criminal know you were on to something, and it all blew up in your face. In that case, a reporter had not just interviewed her dad and other officers about the case, they'd also employed less than ethical tactics and listened to their conversations, even recorded some. And had compromised their safety because of it. Those reporters had been prosecuted, but it didn't bring Erynn's dad back, or solve the case.

"Give me the bare bones," Noah said as he turned onto the main highway that would take them back to Moose Haven proper.

"There was a serial killer in Anchorage about fifteen years ago."

"The link between his victims? Do they know that?"

It had been what he was known for. Some had even dubbed him the "Foster Kid Killer," though the nickname grated so much Erynn tried not to use it. Instead she just thought of the killer as *him*. The unseen presence that had haunted her life in one way or another for years.

"Yes. He was killing foster kids. Some still in high school, some as they aged out of the system."

She felt Noah glance at her, could almost hear the wheels turning in his head. She'd managed to keep her past out of her life in Moose Haven, invent this new identity for herself, where all anyone knew about her past was that she was a trooper.

She'd succeeded. Most days she was proud of herself. Today she knew Noah well enough to understand what a slap in the face it would be to him to learn he hadn't known her as well as he'd thought… She wasn't proud.

She just hurt.

"And you…?"

Still, he asked her to clarify. Erynn took a deep breath. "Yes. I was in foster care for part of that time period. I was adopted the summer before my senior year of high school."

"So you knew the people who were killed."

"Yes." Every single one. Erynn stared out the window, watched the spruce forest as they drove through it on the approach to town. The trees were thick and the woods looked almost like a shelter. If she was Noah's sister Kate and good in the outdoors, maybe she could hide there, manage to survive. But she wasn't Kate and it wasn't an option. She had nowhere to hide and anywhere she ran would only provide temporary security.

The fact that *he* was in Moose Haven proved that.

"Which foster kids was he after specifically?"

Erynn shook her head. "They never…figured that out exactly. Both males and females were killed. No other obvious patterns. One officer had a hunch. But he didn't keep his speculations about that case in a file at work, since they weren't founded on fact, and I don't know where they ended up."

"So we go to Anchorage, ask him and—"

She was already shaking her head. "He's dead, too. And the notes weren't found in any of his personal belongings."

She could feel the tension building, knew the questions were coming. Erynn took a deep breath. "I know because my adoptive mom and I looked. He was my adoptive father."

Noah absorbed Erynn's story, careful not to let his face flinch. She was better at reading him than anyone he knew, and this was one of the times he didn't like that fact.

The killer they were after might have more than one reason to be tracking Erynn down—she wasn't just another former foster kid who might have been in danger. She was the daughter of an investigating officer. Was she in danger because her dad had been killed? Janie had mentioned a police officer losing his life in the investigation, so that meant Erynn's dad…

"He was law enforcement?"

"Yes." She still wouldn't look his way. He knew because he kept glancing over at her as he drove.

"I'm not going to let anything happen to you." Of course, he'd said the same thing to Janie earlier. He'd thought putting her in protective custody would be enough. He'd underestimated the man Erynn was so afraid of. He wouldn't do that again.

"You can't say that."

He didn't argue, knew it was better not to when Erynn was like this. But he meant it. If he had to stop sleeping, follow her around every day, armed, quit his job—

Noah almost jumped in his seat. The thought had come out of nowhere, and made no sense, not when his career gave him access to information that could help figure out who was behind the killings, and could help keep Erynn safe. Nevertheless, the fact that he'd even consider sacrificing the dream he'd always had if it would be enough to keep her safe…

It might be time to stop trying to deceive himself about his feelings for Erynn.

Those emotions were much different than Noah had ever had for any other coworker or any friend. He'd been half in love with Erynn for years and had just avoided it.

He didn't see how he'd be able to entirely sidestep the feelings now. But he'd had to keep them hidden. He had always known there was more to Erynn, just hadn't known exactly what. This was more than he'd expected. And it hurt to know she'd kept it from him.

But he understood. And was going to do everything in his power to make sure that sooner, rather than later, all of this would be in her past, the threat removed. That she could continue with her life, doing what she wanted to do with it without thinking of the implications her choices might have on the madman who was after her.

Noah pulled the car into the back lot at the station. Every vehicle in the department was there and he wished again he had a bigger police force. Not that Moose Haven saw an excess of crime, but if someone drove by and saw that all officers were at the station, it would be an ideal time to get into trouble elsewhere.

He pulled out his cell phone and dialed his brother, who acted as a reserve officer on occasion.

"Tyler, can you come by the station if you get a chance, get a car and just drive around town a bit?" It was more to reassure himself about preventing small crimes than to show the murderer how well equipped they were. Clearly they were not, if he'd been able to waltz into the jail.

Tyler agreed and Noah took a breath.

"Ready?" he asked her when he disconnected.

Erynn was looking out the window. He watched her as she inhaled, squared her shoulders and nodded once. "Ready as I can be."

He stuck close to her as they walked inside, into the chaos. The police department was small but adequate for what they usually needed. Today it seemed crowded, the energy building in a way that made the air feel thick. Too tense. They were already playing defense when they should be on the offense.

He stopped, waited for Erynn at one point. She was still in her uniform and right now looked every inch the trooper she was. Any little chinks that might exist in her armor were not part of her reality in here. She was good at pulling herself together, he'd give her that.

"Where is the body?"

"In the cell. The ME is back there now, getting ready to transport her."

"He can't do that when we haven't had a chance to sketch the scene, process it or anything."

"Officer Hitchcock took care of that. He's back at his desk now, writing it up."

At least he knew that had been handled right. Clay Hitchcock had as many years of law enforcement experience as Noah himself, or at least close. He was also Noah's brother-in-law, married to his sister Summer.

"Let's go talk to Clay," he said to Erynn, motioning with his head at the area with the officers' desks.

Erynn shook her head. "I want to see the crime scene."

"Erynn…"

There it was again. That ridiculous protective instinct toward her that was all too familiar. He had been fighting it for years. Some women liked it when a man wanted to protect them. At least, that was what Noah had gathered from the movies his sisters used to watch and the way he'd seen several of his siblings fall in love. His own personal experience with love was limited. Besides one or two girlfriends in high school that hadn't been serious, he hadn't dated much.

Because the only woman he was interested in dating saw him as a coworker and a friend. Nothing more.

Protective instincts toward her aside, she didn't needed protecting. At least not from the crime scene. If they were going to catch the serial killer responsible, he'd need every good law enforcement mind in town working on the case. And Erynn was one of the best. He couldn't just exclude her from the investigation, which he could only if it really was a conflict of interest for her to investigate a case directly tied to her past. But technically there had been no threat directly to Erynn— at least neither she nor Janie had made him aware of that. The fact that her father had been killed did make her involvement dance close to the line of ethics, but this wasn't a city where police and law enforcement resources were unlimited. She was far enough from the case emotionally to still be involved.

His feelings were going to get in the way of keeping her safe if he wasn't careful. Surely he could make it a few more weeks, till this guy was behind bars, no longer a threat.

It wasn't optional. Noah didn't have a choice. Treating her like any other colleague was the only course of action that was going to work here. So he nodded. "Okay, let's go to the crime scene."

They made their way through the halls. Noah was careful to look for anything that seemed out of place, but nothing caught his attention.

"She was still locked in her cell," one of his officers told him as they walked up to the scene. The man shook his head.

"Do we know how she died yet?"

"Elsie at the front desk mentioned that her lawyer came to see her. I'll go get Clay, he probably knows the most."

As he started to walk away, Noah took in the body on the floor of the cell. It never stopped striking him how once a person had died, they didn't look like they had in life. The body truly ceased to be a person and became a shell, something his law enforcement mentor had taught him when he'd first started.

Janie was pale, her skin lacking the healthy appearance she'd had while alive. Her hair was spread out on the floor behind her, touching the puddle of blood pooled beneath her. She'd been shot in the chest, at very close range.

Noah looked around the cell. The chair was sitting upright. Nothing indicated there had been a struggle.

Was the killer someone she knew? Someone she'd expected to be there to help her?

His mind ran with that thread as he reviewed what the officer had just told him, and he asked, "Janie's lawyer came?" She hadn't been arrested long enough for any lawyer to arrive from Anchorage or even Kenai, whichever place she'd been living. While she could have called a local lawyer…Noah didn't think she had.

The officer nodded.

If his guess was right that the "lawyer" hadn't been one at all, that explained how the killer had gotten inside. Walking in in plain sight. It spoke of a level of overconfidence that could possibly work to their advantage if they could get a step ahead. At the moment it just scared the stupid out of him. "Thanks. Yes, get Hitchcock, please. And do we have video footage?" The cameras in the jail should tell them something, even if the killer had avoided showing his face.

Officer Smith shook his head. "Cameras cut out just before he came in. We've had so many issues with that old system lately that we thought it was a technological glitch."

Noah felt anger stir inside. Not toward his officers. Moose Haven didn't often see crime like this—he understood how they wouldn't have been immediately suspicious—but he hated that evil had won this battle today.

Hated that it felt personal.

"She was sitting in this chair when she was shot, it looks like," Erynn was saying as she moved closer to Janie, tilted her head like she did when she was focused. "See where her body is positioned in relation to the chair? And the blood splatter?"

"Is that significant with past cases or are you just walking through what you see?" Noah forced himself to sound professional, though at the moment he felt anything but. He didn't want Erynn considering victims, blood splatter or anything but keeping herself safe.

But it wasn't his place to keep her out of this. Not when she was already involved so deep her safety was at risk either way.

A second or two passed before she answered. "I think the second? But I'll let you know."

Clay walked into the room just then, his face as sober as Noah felt. They nodded at each other and Noah was as thankful as he had been in the past that Clay had come to Moose Haven. He would need all the help he could get on this one.

"What do we know, Hitchcock?"

The other man shook his head. "I'm trying to go slow, not make assumptions. The fact that someone was able to get into this building and kill someone in our custody… No one even heard a shot."

"He used a suppressor?"

Clay nodded. "That's the working theory."

Noah understood. Hated how Janie's death made him feel. Like he was powerless.

"Has the body been moved?" Noah hadn't wanted to disturb the ME from where he knelt beside the body. The man wore a look of perpetual concern on his face, though Noah guessed if he looked at dead people for a living his face might get stuck like that, too.

"Not yet. Wanted to make sure you had a chance to see the scene if possible. I don't want us to miss anything obvious." Clay's eyes moved to Erynn, who usually would have interrupted several times by now to remind them it was her case, too.

"You okay, Trooper Cooper?" Clay asked.

Erynn barely nodded. "Fine."

Noah spoke at the same time. "She knew the deceased."

Erynn's eyes snapped to him and he saw what she'd tried to hide. She was close to broken by this, looked more fragile than he'd ever seen her. But what really surprised him was the expression of betrayal in her eyes. Because Noah had said she knew the victim? He wanted her on this case, but he couldn't hide anything, couldn't conceal the facts from his own officers.

Still, the way Erynn looked at him, silently begging for more time...

"How?" Clay asked Erynn, but Noah spoke up again.

"High school."

Clay looked like he might ask something else, but the ME interrupted. "There's something underneath her."

All three of them turned as he slid a piece of paper out from beneath her.

"Same color. Same weight. Probably the same pen," Erynn muttered under her breath.

Noah hadn't been expecting the note, but now he remembered Erynn had said that one was always left.

"What does it say? Can you read it?" he asked the ME.

The man read it silently. Frowned. Looked up at them. "It says, *'One more to go.'*"

Erynn's eyes widened and Noah couldn't stop himself this time—he reached for her hand. Held it tight.

The man was driven and his goal was Erynn's death. Something Noah refused to let happen.

FOUR

Erynn did not remember walking from the crime scene to Noah's office, but there she was. Sitting in a chair across from his desk, blinking.

She had precious little time to get her head back into the game if she was going to make a difference before she was taken off the case. Because as sure as she knew anything else, she knew her days working it were numbered. She had personal connections everywhere, and while she disagreed with protocol suggesting it would make her less effective on the case, it wasn't worth arguing over.

Instead she just needed to work fast, find as many leads as possible to turn over to whomever was put on the case after she was relieved.

And then work the case on her own time, quietly. Because she owed her dad that.

"You've got to stop staring. Blink or something."

She did, almost without thinking; her eyes were drier than she'd noticed and needed the moisture. She blinked again.

"Erynn…"

The way Noah's voice trailed off was almost too

much for her. Years, she had tried to stay on the edges of the tight-knit community of people who made up Moose Haven. Years, he'd fought her on it, pulled her not just into the town, but into the inner circle his family and friends occupied. She'd told herself it couldn't hurt and yet here, at this moment, it seemed it could hurt a lot.

"Don't, Noah." It was enough to get her to look up, focus. "You can't talk to me like that, okay?" Like she was a victim. Which she was, or might be at any moment, but right now she was still a law enforcement officer, wasn't going to give up the responsibility that came with that until someone forcefully benched her.

"You've been through a lot."

Yeah, the story of her life. She'd tired of the pity early on in her "career" as a foster kid, especially because that didn't give her a home of her own, didn't give her the stability that so many kids her age had and took for granted. Though she knew Noah didn't mean it that way, he didn't know what the words made her think of.

"We're both about to go through a lot more and people in Moose Haven could suffer if we don't get this case under control."

"This case meaning the Ice Maiden case?"

Erynn shivered. She'd always hated that name, too, as much as she'd hated the "Foster Kid Killer" nickname for the serial killer who had terrorized and marked her teen years. Why did departments, the media, whoever did it, name killers, name cases? Criminals didn't deserve the notoriety, and she disliked the way it glamorized them.

Still, she understood; how else were they going to refer to cases? So she just nodded, fought to get her emotions under control. "Yes, the Ice Maiden case. We need to go back and rework it. Because Janie coming out of hiding, telling us about that…"

"There was nothing there."

"Clearly there was. Because the woman we thought had died hadn't, but now has, and we don't know who is up in that glacier crevasse. That could present another lead."

He didn't say anything, to his credit. But she heard the things he wasn't saying. They'd had a team of people working with them when the case had been hot initially, and they still hadn't been able to find many leads on who it could be.

Was it someone who was now local to Moose Haven? Someone who had tracked her here and decided to terrorize her more? Erynn knew from her profiling classes the way a serial killer's mind worked. It wasn't impossible to suggest that the killer had become fixated on her years ago.

Still, it was all just conjecture. She was tired of that. She needed facts.

"Okay. So you're telling me you're convinced that the Ice Maiden death wasn't an accident, wasn't a disappearance, but is instead connected to…" Noah trailed off, his voice fading away and giving Erynn the opportunity to explain out loud the suspicions she'd always had.

"The Foster Kid Killer."

"And you believe this because Janie was in the foster system?"

"Yes, and so was Michelle."

"Michelle is the woman who warned Janie to be careful, right before Janie disappeared and we discovered the body in the glacier."

Erynn nodded. Waited a minute. "We have to get to her, Noah. We have to know for sure if it's Michelle or if chasing leads on the body in the glacier will just be pulling our attention away from an active serial killer."

Noah's brow furrowed, his face serious in consideration. "It's December, Erynn. Accessing the body we left on the glacier is going to be even more impossible now. It's buried under who knows how many layers of snow and the wind on the glacier at this time of year…"

"We have to try, Noah. Every single angle."

She was right. She knew it and he did, too, but that didn't make this any easier. That case had almost cost them so much, years ago. He hadn't been sure either one of them would make it through, and now it was back, had never gone away.

If he was a runner, he'd leave town, build a career somewhere else, do something else. He had hated the Ice Maiden case with every fiber of his being because it was a nightmare come true—a woman went into the Alaskan wilderness and turned up dead. The news had overpublicized it, used it as a cautionary tale against backcountry hiking alone even once law enforcement had declared the death accidental, but doubts had niggled at Noah's mind even then, and an oppressive heaviness had been present during the entire time they worked the case. Now that he knew it involved Erynn personally, he hated it more.

He glanced over at her again. What he should do was call her superiors at the trooper post, get her moved out of town and off this case. Protocol probably dictated it. But to what end? She'd be farther from him, where he had no choice but to let someone else try to keep her safe. And the idea of someone else failing...

Besides, much as he'd sparred with her over case-working strategies the last few years, as many times as they'd ribbed each other, they'd worked well as a team, and he needed her. Did not want to tackle this case *again* at all, much less without Erynn.

"Okay, you're right."

Her face was the brightest he'd seen it tonight, that look she got when he admitted she had a point. Still, she was too pale. Someone had threatened to kill her tonight, someone who might have been after her for well over a decade.

"I do like hearing you say that." Her voice was lighter, like she was trying to make the best of a bad situation. While he appreciated her optimism, wanted her to relax a little, he wasn't planning to follow suit.

Noah couldn't relax anytime soon. Not if he wanted to keep Erynn alive.

"Most of the files for the Ice Maiden case were digitized, so it shouldn't be too hard to pull up everything we had on it. The evidence is still in cold storage." He opened his computer, glanced up when he saw movement, and watched as Erynn dragged a chair to the back of his desk. She paused just as she was about to sit. "May I? Sit here, I mean?"

He nodded. On all the cases they'd worked together, either he or Erynn had pursued a lead and it had been clear "whose" case it was. This was the first time they had sat on the same side of any desk. He nodded again, hoping she understood it was fine, but unable to say anything. Was this the closest he'd been to her physically? They'd ridden in patrol cars together, hers, his.

But she was scooting her chair closer now, close enough he could sense her shampoo, which smelled like the beach. Coconut or something like it.

Years. He'd ignored this crush for *years*. Worked around it, denied it even to himself. He had to hang on for however long it took to put this guy behind bars. He owed it to Erynn.

"So where should we start? I'm assuming you have an opinion."

Her behavior was almost back to normal and he was panicked at the idea that he could have lost her tonight.

He had to shake this insecurity, needed to be the man he usually was in this office. Capable. Confident.

"We need to start at square one. It's going to give us more than if we just try to figure out where our mistakes were."

"Of course. Because if those had been obvious, we'd have seen them the first time."

The program loaded and Noah pulled up the files they needed. Decided to read out loud, not because Erynn couldn't see over his shoulder, but they both were the type who talked things out.

"'Jane Doe, discovered by hikers on the glacier three and a half years ago, on July 3. Initially it was assumed a hiker had misstepped and died as a result of her injuries, but the lack of gear observed near the hiker eventually turned it into a missing persons investigation with a suspicion she'd been murdered.'"

He stopped reading, looked over at Erynn, who was still closer than she'd ever been. But just as out of his reach. "That whole time, did you know?"

"Know what?"

"That she was a victim of the person…"

Erynn shook her head. "No, the body was reported. I knew only what you did, assumed the same things."

"At what point did you suspect there was more to it than the rest of us knew?"

"Keep reading."

"'Trooper Erynn Cooper and Moose Haven Police Chief Noah Dawson investigated the scene and put out a missing persons report. Janie Davis, reported missing in the Kenai Peninsula area on July 1, was last seen in Seward, which also has a glacier that flows out of Harding Icefield, where the body was discovered—'"

"There." Erynn broke in. "As soon as Janie's name came up, I knew."

"Did you assume the body was hers?"

"Yes." She said it without hesitation and he believed her. She'd never given him a reason not to. It was becoming clearer to him that she hadn't been generous in her details about her past. He understood now it had been intentional on her part. She had kept it from him, from all of them. To protect herself from a killer? From being ashamed of where she'd been?

Noah didn't know and, if he didn't know, he couldn't fix it. He hated not being able to fix things.

"Do you want coffee?" He was exhausted. His mind felt fuzzy around the edges; hers had to, also. Bringing coffee was something he could do, and a quick trip to the break room would let him check in with some of his officers on anything they had discovered from the crime scene in the cell.

"Right now?" She glanced at her watch. "It's past ten."

"And you're too young to have rules about when you drink caffeine." He stood and walked to the door but stopped. "Unless you wanted to try to get some sleep? I can keep pulling up old details and you could catch a nap in the chairs, or maybe on the sofa."

"Not happening."

"Sleep might be good." He could only manage a half-hearted attempt to convince her. He couldn't imagine her sleeping anytime in the next few hours, at least not well. If he were her, he wouldn't want to try.

Erynn bit her lip, a frown clouding her features. "You know exactly what I'll see if I close my eyes. And you'd want me to try?"

"No." This time he didn't hesitate. "You need coffee."

Noah opened the door, saw Tyler walking by. His brother had a job at the family's lodge, running the place, but he'd humored Noah and gone to the trooper academy to become law enforcement certified so he could help out at the department when there were special circumstances. Tonight qualified.

"Tyler." Noah nodded at his office. "Can you stay with Erynn while I get us some coffee?"

"Of course." Tyler stepped up to the door, stopped to look at Noah and let the door shut between them and Erynn. "How is she?" He'd lowered his voice, which Noah appreciated, but he still wasn't comfortable talking about Erynn like she wasn't there, or worse, like she was some random victim who needed to be treated with kid gloves. Yeah, Erynn wouldn't appreciate it at all.

"She's fine. Considering. She'll be better when I get her some coffee." Noah blew out a breath, turned back to his brother. "Look, I'm sorry."

"It's okay, I get it. It's hard."

Noah raised his eyebrows. "You get it?"

"Does Emma showing up in town with someone after

her ring a bell? I understand. I'll make sure Erynn's okay while you're gone." Tyler was implying…

"You aren't saying I have the kind of feelings for Erynn that you have—"

"Just get the coffee. I shouldn't have said anything."

But it wasn't like everyone with eyes didn't know. Noah heard what Tyler wasn't saying. His feelings for Erynn had been obvious to everyone but her for years. He'd never acted on them because Erynn was…she was too special to lose if she didn't feel the same way. And he'd always felt her hesitation, the way she held people at arm's length, and he had not wanted to make her uncomfortable by trying to get closer to her if that was not what she wanted. Now he wondered if he'd lost his chance with her altogether, if he should have been honest with her. But it was too late to change anything now, or to hide his feelings from the town. Noah did not bother to defend himself this time, did not bother to play dumb, just nodded and headed for the break room.

"So, what did you learn while you were gone?"

Erynn tried not to sound too interested, but every cell in her body was on high alert, ready to charge forward into battle against the killer. If only she had a face, a name, something to make him more substance than just a terror who haunted her dreams, killed her friends, her family.

She wanted a fair fight. She couldn't have that if she didn't know who he was.

"I got you coffee. That's why I was gone." He handed it to her and she took a sip. Strong, with just a tiny bit of half-and-half. She didn't deserve to have a friend who knew her so well—especially when she usually drank it black. It was healthier that way, for one. For another, proving herself as a woman in a male-dominated profession dictated that she take every opportunity to show herself capable. Strong. She felt like black coffee made a statement, and had drunk it that way since she'd graduated from the trooper academy. But half-and-half was a guilty pleasure, one that felt like a treat.

And Noah always remembered. She was starting to realize he remembered everything about her, and that knowledge made her feel seen. It was either exhilarating or terrifying: Erynn didn't know which. She had spent too much time hoping she'd blend in, just be *normal*. Average. She hadn't even dated much because she hadn't wanted to take the risk that being close to her would put someone else in danger. She'd never felt fully free from the threat that the Foster Kid Killer would return.

She wished her instincts had been wrong this time.

"We both know you didn't just get coffee." She took another sip. "Though thank you, this is really good."

"I did talk to some of the other officers who were here, but I didn't learn much. Everything they know is what we know."

"He didn't leave any evidence here, either." She heard the flatness in her voice, couldn't quite fix it. She'd wondered for years if the killer was law enforcement himself, but her dad hadn't believed he was, hadn't believed anyone he worked with in Anchorage would have done the things he'd done. Still, the murderer knew more than an average person about how the crime scene process worked. He was smart. Otherwise they'd have caught him by now.

The chances he was going to be stupid now, after a

decade to learn more, plan more? They weren't good. Erynn wished it wasn't true, but she wasn't going to delude herself into thinking positively for no reason.

"He didn't, but we're going to find him."

She had been the sunshine on Noah's shoulder before when he was having a hard time with a case, knew full well she'd helped keep him sane when his sisters had been through dangerous situations in the last year and a half. But having him try to cheer her up? She couldn't handle it right now. She was only up for full reality, which wasn't so sunny.

"I don't see how we can."

Noah turned to her, didn't say anything. She dared him to, dared him to lie to her to try to make the whole thing sound more likely than it was.

He didn't. Instead he just nodded. Turned back to the computer.

He might have confidence, but she had none. And he didn't even mind.

Everything in her wished she could hang on to him and not let him go, make him promise they'd be friends forever, but she didn't have much longer in Moose Haven. She'd already had a longer tenure here than she should have because of department changeover and how assignments shook out. But in a year or less she would be leaving Moose Haven for another posting.

She'd walk out of his life; he'd find someone else to make coffee for, to encourage, and she'd be alone, like she'd always been. It wasn't fair. However, Erynn had learned at an early age that life wasn't. Had had it reinforced for her often since.

"Here's an angle we can work. As you said, we suspect now that Michelle Holt was the woman who was really killed on the glacier. Will working from there lead us to him?"

"I doubt it."

"It was rhetorical. Maybe don't answer if you don't have something positive to say, okay?"

Erynn didn't say anything. She just sipped her coffee, let Noah keep talking to her, or himself, or whomever he was talking to.

"We're going to solve this, Erynn. I promise."

Erynn swallowed hard. It wasn't the first time she'd heard the words. The last time, she had known the person cared about her, known he'd meant them.

And then he'd ended up dead.

She couldn't let that happen to Noah. Or to her.

FIVE

Noah checked his phone. No message from Erynn in the last couple of hours. He checked his watch: 3:00 a.m. Well, that would explain why. They had wrapped up at the department not long after he'd brought the coffee in. Erynn had said she'd wanted to try to get some sleep. But Noah wouldn't be surprised if she'd mostly wanted a break from him and his misplaced optimism. He could use one, also, but giving up was not an option.

You still okay? He typed out the words in a text message, made himself set the phone down rather than wait for a reply. His sister Summer, Clay's wife, had called and insisted Erynn stay with them rather than return to her house. Noah had been planning to post one of his officers at her house, even though he didn't have the manpower, but this option was better. He trusted Clay to keep both Erynn and Summer safe if anything went wrong, and Summer would keep him updated if anything changed. He'd walked her out to Clay and Summer's car, the winter darkness weighing on him. The town's holiday decorations hung on every streetlight—candles, holly, Christmas trees made of lights—and their joyfulness mocked him. This was supposed to be a season of happiness, wasn't it?

Instead Erynn was afraid for her life. And Noah felt powerless to stop it.

It didn't feel much like Christmas.

Logically, Noah knew sleep would help his mind-set. It wouldn't erase the threat, but it might bring clarity. He should really get some rest.

She's okay, right? He typed the text to Summer and sent it before he could let his good sense change his mind. This time he really did set the phone down and lie back on his pillow.

The phone buzzed.

He sat up to read the message from Erynn. I'm fine. Go to sleep, Noah.

He exhaled. *God, help me.* He had worked hundreds of cases in the years he'd been serving Moose Haven but nothing had touched him this closely. Not even when his sisters were in danger.

Erynn was different. He was different with her. And in all these years of working together, he'd never told her how much she meant to him. He couldn't now, either. He had to stay focused, had to avoid giving her any reason to elude him because, while he had a case to solve, the fact was he didn't trust anyone else to keep her safe the way he would. Wasn't sure anyone cared the way he did.

He pulled the covers up, let himself nod off. He wouldn't do either of them any good exhausted.

When he woke again it was past five in the morning. Late enough to start work.

He checked his phone to find two messages, one from Summer. She's fine. Seriously, she's going to know how you feel if you keep hovering.

Yeah, Erynn might not know about his feelings for her, but there was a good chance she was the only one in Moose Haven.

The next message was from Erynn. Sent five minutes ago, probably what had woken him. I'm going up to Harding Icefield. Are you coming?

Noah typed out a reply. Stay put. I'll be right there.

He showered more quickly than usual, changed into fresh clothes and headed outside to his car, locking his front door as he did so and then pausing to look at the deck.

He'd forgotten to have someone process his front porch for evidence. Chances were slim the killer had left any evidence besides the note itself, which he had taken into the police department—it had come up clean, no prints or useful DNA samples. Still, he should look around.

The two rocking chairs on the porch looked relatively undisturbed, as did everything else.

He slid out his phone and texted Clay Hitchcock, the man on his team with the most crime scene training, and asked him to come by to see if there was any forensic evidence Noah wasn't seeing.

Clay texted On my way and arrived in less than five minutes.

Noah debated staying with him.

"You look like you're on edge." Clay stated the obvious as he dusted the table for prints, sprinkling the deep black dust over the surface.

"Erynn's threatening to investigate without me. She didn't say anything to you?"

He shook his head. "Go. I'll call you if I find anything."

Noah did not need to be told twice. Indecision defeated, he hurried to his car and drove to Clay and Summer's cabin on the edge of the family's property about a five-minute drive away.

Her car was gone. Summer had sure better be with her. His sister was not trained in anything, but she was an athlete and she'd had a serial killer after her once. Anything was better than Erynn being alone.

Noah left his car running, knocked on the door just in case.

No one answered. As he'd expected.

Stubborn. She was pure stubbornness, that's all there was to it, and if it got her killed…

Well, it just couldn't. Because Noah didn't know how he'd manage to keep living if anything happened to her. She'd leave that big a hole in his everyday life and she didn't even know it. If she was okay, if he found her… He wasn't going to be able to keep quiet for much longer. Bad timing or not.

He climbed back into the car and drove up to Harding Edge Road, which would take him to the base of the mountain, to Moose Haven's Harding Icefield Trailhead. The parking lot had one car in it. Erynn's.

A wave of hot anger washed over him and Noah gritted his teeth. He climbed out of his car, slammed the door and started toward the trailhead.

"Hey."

The voice had come from behind him. Erynn. He whipped his head around.

"Are you going to wait for us?" She had the driver's-side window down, was leaning halfway out of it and smiling.

He couldn't understand the second part. What was there to smile about? He tried to shrug off some of the anger that had built, but more than likely it wouldn't all dissipate until he'd had a chance to burn off energy on the trail. Hiking was his favorite way to deal with stress. Not fast, running nonsense like Summer enjoyed. Not the risky high-stakes hikes Kate was used to after all of her Search-and-Rescue work. Just hikes. Alone or with his brother, Tyler. But mostly alone.

"I'm waiting." What else was there to say? She'd scared the tar out of him, coming here without waiting for him. While he was thankful nothing had happened to her in the trailhead parking lot, it had still been foolish.

The passenger-side door opened and Summer climbed out, dressed for hiking. Noah was already shaking his head. "Absolutely not."

"I didn't want her to come out here alone, Noah. It was the only choice I had." She shrugged.

"No." He didn't know if the two women thought they could take him on, but this was his investigation—even more so than Erynn's, since her time on it would likely be limited once her superiors at the trooper station realized how close she was to it personally. "Besides, I'm with her now. I don't want you in danger, too."

"Should I drive Erynn's car back?" Summer looked to Erynn, who had climbed out of the car and was digging in the trunk.

"Works for me." Noah looked at Erynn, dared her to argue. Instead she nodded. "If you don't mind, that would be great. But wait until Clay can come up here to meet you."

Noah saw where she was going, already had his phone out to call Clay.

"He's sending one of the other officers since he was out at my place."

* * *

If Erynn had the kind of vision that enabled her to
see people's emotions, there would be literal waves of
anger rolling off Noah. They'd been hiking for a solid
hour and he'd said nothing to her, just stuck so close
that she'd bumped into him more than once and the way
he'd reacted was even more confusing than his anger.
When their hands had brushed, he'd made eye contact
with her, held it for a moment too long, and something
had shivered inside her all the way to her toes.

Ridiculous. She had known for ages that she had a
small crush on Noah, but nothing she felt for him was
real or substantial enough to weather the perpetual storm
that was her life. She had no business experiencing tin-
gling in her toes, or anywhere else, because of the man.

For now what she needed was to convince him that
she felt nothing for him. And to focus on figuring out
how to keep everyone around her safe while she finally
pinpointed the identity of the man who'd haunted her
dreams for more than a decade.

Noah stopped, too close for Erynn to stop fully,
and she ran into him. In half a second he'd turned and
caught her by the upper arms.

"What is with you?" She couldn't stop her frustration from exploding.

"I thought I heard something."

"We're in the woods in the winter. You probably
heard a moose."

He still hadn't let her go, still had his hands on her
arms, and every cell in her was aware of his touch.

Erynn cleared her throat, looked at her arms, one at
a time. Back at Noah, who was looking at her. "Are you
thinking of letting me go?"

"Erynn…"

The way his voice trailed off, husky with emotion, made her know that their time limit for ignoring whatever was between them was about to run out. And the timing couldn't be worse.

For years their easygoing banter had been one of the highlights of her life. Being free to fall in love with Noah, able to live a normal life without looking over her shoulder…

Erynn couldn't think of anything she'd like more. But she didn't have that freedom right now. Letting Noah get closer to her would only put a target on his back. She couldn't do that to him.

Shaking her head, she pulled backward just enough that Noah released her. She had known he would. He'd never be the kind of man who continued an advance, even an innocent touch like that, when it was unwelcome.

"We've got to get up there and find her body."

"I think I'm in love with you."

Their voices harmonized as their words clashed. Badly.

Erynn blinked. She'd feared he'd want to talk about whatever *this* was between them, but she'd never have imagined he'd go this far. Her palms felt wet and she brushed them on her pants, looking away from Noah as she waited. Should she say something first? Would he?

Her traitorous heart fluttered and she struggled to catch her breath. Never had she fought attraction to anyone like this.

But she couldn't let him love her. Not now. His timing was awful.

"I'm sorry…" Noah started and Erynn felt her pulse slow. A mistake. He knew it had been a mistake.

He continued. "I know this is awful timing. I shouldn't have said it. But I meant it. Every word. And sometime we need to talk about it."

Erynn fought to unscramble her thoughts, but it was too much. The man after her. Seeing Janie again after so many years and finding her dead. Noah loved her. Her life was in danger.

She could not let the memory of her father down. Not after she'd sacrificed so much to get here, to be in the position to do something to help catch the man she still believed was responsible for his death.

"I can't talk about this now, Noah. I have to find out who killed my dad and the others."

Noah nodded slowly, his face resigned to her answer. Erynn swallowed hard, wished she could take that look off his face. "Listen, when this is over…" But she looked away as she said it. Even when this was over, she wouldn't be in a place where she could afford to fall in love with Noah. In the next year or two she'd be leaving and his family and entire life was in Moose Haven. Even if that wasn't an issue, Erynn didn't know that she'd ever get married.

Her birth parents never had, but her biological father had broken her mom's heart time and time again. That had probably been what led to her biological mom's downward spiral, drugs and ending up on the street, losing custody of Erynn.

No, Noah wasn't cut from the same cloth… He was a better man.

Nevertheless, he was still a man, still not worth trusting with her entire life and self-worth. Not if children were doomed to repeat their parents' mistakes.

Because Erynn had no desire to spend the rest of her life broken because of a man. Like her mom had.

"Okay, when this is over. We'll talk then."

She raised her eyebrows, surprised at his sudden agreement. Noah liked to be right. Not that she could blame him. So did she. "You mean it? We won't discuss it at all now?"

"Discuss what?" He blinked, his eyes shining almost with mischief.

To be able to feel that lighthearted...Erynn would give almost anything. But there wasn't any chance of that, so she smiled. "Thank you."

Noah started forward on the trail again and Erynn followed. She considered herself to be in good shape, but her thighs burned from the uphill climb, one of the toughest the area had to offer, even in the summer. Now, in December, she and Noah were both wearing Kahtoola MICROspikes for traction, and each step took more effort than it should to dig her boots into the snow and ice to make sure she didn't fall.

Because the last thing she needed, besides finally being killed by a man who'd wanted her dead for half of her life, was to fall down and have Noah rescuing a damsel in distress.

She did her own rescuing, thank you very much.

Noah didn't seem to have much to say anymore, and Erynn felt herself relax a little with every minute he was quiet. They'd had such an easy working relationship, and yes, she'd seen more than once over the last few years how it could easily sneak into more. So very easily.

But she couldn't let it. For either of their sakes. Because even if Erynn wasn't afraid to risk her heart the way her mom had, she knew her past had left her with an entire airport truckful of baggage. It might not be true for everyone who'd been in foster care as a teen, but it was true in her life.

Noah deserved better.

Another strike against them.

She should not be thinking of Noah at all right now. She should be thinking like the victim whose final resting place they were going to see. The Ice Maiden had taken this trail before she was killed. Erynn looked around, tried to see the area through the eyes of someone living her last day.

Had Michelle come up here of her own power? Been brought up here to die? They'd never been able to answer either question to Erynn's satisfaction. Erynn readjusted the straps of her backpack, tired of the way it was slamming into her lower back.

Backpack.

If the Ice Maiden had come up on her own, she'd have been prepared for the hike. Was there a backpack somewhere they had overlooked when they'd investigated before? As fast as the thought entered her mind, Erynn dismissed it. They had canvassed the entire area. Even if they'd missed something, it wouldn't be discoverable anymore. People or animals would likely have moved it, as this trail was fairly well traveled in the summer and home to quite a few bears.

She took another couple steps up the mountain, dug her spikes into the ice. As she did, her mind kept working, stumbling down a mental trail she thought might have merit...

"Noah." He turned to look at her, the hope on his face enough to tell her he was wishing she would discuss something personal rather than the case. She decided ignoring that was the best course of action, feeling her jaw clench in resistance to the way she knew she was hurting him. "What if she had a backpack with her?"

"You know we looked for anything like that."

Erynn shook her head. "What if it's under the body?"

Noah stopped walking, seemed to consider the question. At least it looked like it with the way he angled his head. "It's possible."

"We're going to have to find a way to recover the body, now that the case is back open." At least it was winter and though it would take more work, recovery was safer for those working. There had been snow still, that June, the snow pack around the glacier deemed too unstable to recover the body at the time. Now it should be stable, though uncovering the body would be more difficult.

Now things had changed. Everything had changed.

"You aren't going down to that glacier."

"I didn't ask to." The thought had crossed Erynn's mind, but she knew there were people who were better equipped to handle that aspect of the investigation. Her skills in the backcountry weren't bad, but they were limited to when she actually had solid ground beneath her feet. Glaciers, especially crevasses and ice caves, were quiet dangers, but could turn deadly easily enough.

In fact, the person who'd initially called in the body's discovery had assumed the death had been an accident. Until they'd investigated and found signs that could have indicated a struggle in the area.

When missing persons reports had indicated it might be Janie, Erynn had been crushed.

He would never stop coming after them.

Even now she had to gulp a breath down, focus on expanding her lungs with enough air to keep her heart from skipping beats, like it did sometimes when she was nervous. A benign condition, the cardiologist she'd seen had assured her, but irritating enough. Who was she, a heroine in a romance novel, that her heart would dare to do something as dramatic as flutter out of rhythm?

No, Erynn wasn't made for romance. Any relationship she'd tried to have as a teen hadn't gone anywhere— she was too closed off to let someone get to know her easily and most boys hadn't wanted to put in the effort. Besides, her parents' history should serve as a warning to her—their failures were probably genetic. She'd settle for being friends with people who'd found their happily-ever-afters—enough of them certainly had in the last couple of years. The entire Dawson family, besides Noah, had paired off in twenty-four months or less and several other friends from town had gotten married, too.

If it was something in the water, Erynn would start drinking bottled. She had no desire to take a risk like that, had no time for it anyway.

Because her entire life from the age of sixteen on had been about one day finding the man who'd killed her friends and her father.

She wasn't going to give up now. Not when she finally had a lead to chase.

SIX

Noah inhaled to catch his breath when they finally reached the top of the trail. The mountain pass stretched out in front of them, the glacier field vast and covered in December snow.

If they were able to remember where the body had been, despite it being three years later with a fresh layer of snow, it would prove they had someone on their side.

Noah had never doubted God's presence, not the way he knew some people struggled with it. No, God was real, present, all-powerful. Those aspects of faith were so ingrained into his consciousness that he doubted he'd ever waver on those points. But God being full of love and caring?

Eh, Noah could never be sure. He sort of tried to live the best he could, to trust God for his salvation since he was aware of the fact that it was by grace alone, but he assumed he was responsible for sorting out his own life. The details were Noah's to handle. Surely, God had bigger issues to deal with.

Like that of the death of a woman who lay somewhere in front of them. Ten yards, twenty yards? Less? The topography of the glacier wasn't static, and the changes in the last few years could be numerous.

He'd reacted to Erynn's desire to come up here. Had he been thinking clearly, he'd have gotten a team together, found some people skilled in glacier travel and been ready for the body recovery. There was no need to be there until then.

Noah turned, about to tell Erynn they had come for nothing. But she wasn't beside him anymore. She was ten feet away, closer to the glacier's edge than he was, thought her feet were still on solid ground, underneath a layer of snow. At least he thought so. She was staring out ahead of her and the expression on her face was...

Crushed. That was the only word that came to mind. In that second, when she must not have realized he was watching, he saw more vulnerability than he had in the entire time he'd known her. Saw the way the years of feeling hunted, of wondering when her worst nightmare was going to return, had taken their toll.

He stepped closer. She jerked at the noise his spikes made on the ice, turned toward him, her usual confident mask perfectly in place again.

Noah wanted her to trust him enough to be without it. Didn't want her to hurt. But if she did, he wanted to know. Wanted her to want that, too.

He needed to hike. Alone. Sort out all these feelings and figure out why a secret he'd kept hidden for years had finally demanded *today* to be let out.

And did she feel the same? She hadn't said anything to give him hope, but she hadn't denied anything, either.

"We need to get a team up here," he said aloud to remind himself to focus and to give him something to say to Erynn, a reason to have stepped closer.

She nodded, her eyes leaving him and going to the

expanse of snow and ice. "I was realizing that, too. It was foolish to come up here."

"Not entirely. We got to see the scene again, remember what it's like. We'll be better prepared because of it."

A half smile quirked at the corner of her mouth, her lips red in the cold and distracting him from what he should be thinking about. He reminded himself her safety was at stake and brought his mind back to where it should be. "You're trying to make me feel better since it was my decision to be hasty and come up here."

"Maybe." He wasn't going to deny it. Noah shrugged. "It's true, though. Nothing's wasted." Something his parents had always said. Although they had always said, "Nothing's wasted with God." He'd never been sure exactly what they'd meant, but had nodded like he knew he was supposed to rather than ask for an explanation.

"Thanks, Noah." Something in her tone made him look up at her, but if her face had given any indication of her feelings, it was gone now.

Noah made himself smile. Act natural. But he knew nothing between them would ever be the way it had been.

"Let's go for now," he said, and she didn't argue.

They reached the trailhead faster than he would have expected, and a cursory check of the car said it hadn't been tampered with. There was always an outside chance and Noah did not like to take risks.

He waited until Erynn was safely inside the car before he climbed in, taking one last look at the empty parking lot, listening to the winter wind howl through the open space, since even the parking lot itself was above the tree line.

"Everything okay?" she asked as he pulled out of the gravel parking lot.

The woman he loved would prefer not to know that he loved her, and someone wanted her dead.

It was a loaded question to try to answer. So he just didn't. Let Erynn assume what she wanted.

She did not comment. Apparently didn't care enough to bridge the gap of his silence. Noah didn't know why he was surprised.

The drive back to town went quickly and Noah hurried Erynn inside the Moose Haven Police Department with him.

"We need to get the team up there to retrieve the body as soon as possible," Erynn muttered as they walked inside. Thinking out loud wasn't unusual for her, Noah knew, especially when she was deep in a case mentally and she was either alone or surrounded by other people in law enforcement.

"I know." They needed the lead, that part didn't need discussing or affirming. Besides, a December storm was blowing in, and the body, which would be difficult enough to locate now after years of settling snow, would be nearly impossible to find in the blinding storm forecasters were predicting for this weekend. They couldn't afford to sit around for days waiting for the recovery to take place. This was their best shot. They needed to take it.

Recovering the body years ago, when it was only a recovery effort, had been deemed too dangerous. It wasn't uncommon in Alaska for bodies to stay in their final resting places in the backcountry if it was deemed too unsafe for volunteers to retrieve them without risk to themselves. Now that they had reason to believe that the Ice Maiden had been murdered, retrieving the body was a higher priority.

Erynn walked straight to Noah's office, like she owned the place. He didn't blame her for her confidence; she'd been there so many times over the years it made sense that she was as at ease here as in the trooper building. And it made something squeeze in Noah's heart every time. Which was ridiculous. What, she didn't feel comfortable enough to trust him with her personal life and stories of her past, but she felt comfortable in his office? He should smack himself on the head, a Gibbs-from-*NCIS*-style slap. Her being relaxed here did not mean anything for their chances of a relationship. They had no shot at that.

A fact Noah couldn't quite get his entire heart to believe, not when he'd never felt this way about anyone before. Didn't anticipate feeling this way about anyone else again.

Most women he knew, while lovely people, just didn't…match him the way Erynn did. She wasn't intimidated by his take-charge personality—she had one of her own to match. They fit, the two of them. It had been obvious to him almost from when they first met that she was special. Out of his league, too good for him, gorgeous beyond reason.

Erynn cleared her throat and he looked up, met her eyes. Thankfully he didn't see anything in her expression that indicated she'd developed an ability to read his thoughts. He might have tipped his hand a bit with her, but he didn't want to confess to the full depth of his feelings, let her know that he was convinced she was "the one." He did have some measure of pride and that rejection this morning had been more than enough for him.

"Who are you thinking of asking to retrieve the body?" Erynn asked as she settled into a chair across from his desk. Noah walked behind the desk and picked up his work phone, started to dial.

"I'm going to talk to Kate to see if she can coordinate an effort."

Erynn raised her eyebrows. "The same Kate who is living in Anchorage?"

"She'll know who my best contact is down here."

"How about the Search-and-Rescue guy who took her place?"

Noah shrugged. "I just want to confirm with her what the best course of action is. She was the best at her job, the best anywhere around. I still can't believe she gave all that up. And don't fully understand why she did. Moving to Anchorage, sure, but changing careers?"

He dialed Kate's number, explained the situation and listened as she gave her recommendations. She sounded happy. Noah was glad for that, even if she was the first of the Dawson siblings to move out of Moose Haven. It was a strange reality that was going to take some adjusting, but Noah knew she was where she should be.

A cop. Living in Anchorage. Married to his old friend Micah Reed.

Who'd have guessed any of it? Life could be funny sometimes.

He told his sister goodbye and ended the call.

Erynn spoke up immediately. "About Kate and what you said earlier about her giving up her job here…"

Noah waited.

"I think sometimes people have more behind their decisions than we know. And with how private your sister is? I doubt she'd have explained her reasons for switching careers, even to you guys, but I'm sure she probably had them."

Noah opened his mouth to argue, closed it again as he realized Erynn could be right. But, more important for his situation right now, Erynn was telling him something true about her, giving him a glimpse into how her mind worked.

It was a gift he wasn't planning to refuse.

"Thanks for explaining." He met Erynn's eyes, held them even as he could tell she wanted to look away. "I didn't know."

Erynn looked away, brushed a strand of dark red hair behind her ear and looked back at him, her face a mask of generic professionalism. "So what did she tell you?"

"Same thing you guessed. She said the guy who took her place, Sam Tomlinson, is good at his job and can do what we need him to do."

"She didn't give you a time frame, did she? For how long recovery will take?"

The way she shifted in her chair wasn't lost on him. Neither was the way she looked away as she asked the question, the way her voice sounded too casual, like she didn't have so much riding on the answer.

"She didn't. But she told me she knew Sam would understand we're under a lot of pressure to do this as fast as possible."

"But safely. I don't want anyone else to die because of…"

Because of her? It was not hard for Noah to guess how she'd have finished that sentence, but he was already shaking his head. "Erynn."

"Don't, Noah. I don't want to hear it, okay? I'm not like your sisters. There's no amount of reassurance in

the world that could make me 'bounce back'—" her tone
and the air quotes she used were filled with sarcasm
"—the way they did from the tragedies they've been
through. I'm sorry each of them had to go through that,
you know I am, but this is my life, this has been my life
for decades. It's not something happening to me right
now, this killer, being hunted by him… This is so big a
part of who I am that I wouldn't know how to let it go
if I tried, all right?"

She stood, shook her head. "So please stop thinking
you can fix this. Catch the guy, by all means, but even
that won't fix this. Not entirely."

"Where are you going?" Noah asked.

"I need to go to my office."

"I'll come with you."

She opened her mouth to argue and apparently
thought better of it.

Noah couldn't appreciate his small victory, though,
because the way her shoulders fell told him all he
needed to know about her views on the case.

In Erynn's mind, she had already lost.

Erynn didn't know what she needed in her office,
didn't know why she felt the need to be there, unless
it was the fact that it was more "her" turf than Noah's.
She'd felt off-balance around him all morning.

Years of her life were chasing her down, like a bad
dream she couldn't wake from, and she was going to
have to face her past head-on. His confession about
his feelings was the last thing she needed to deal with
right now. Sure, she'd wondered. Okay, she'd more than
wondered. She had known for years that he'd be a very
easy man to fall for. He cared about people around him,

loved truth and justice. He was a man of faith, and while hers had wavered some over the years, it still mattered to her. If ever there had been someone who could show her how to live out her faith when times were hard, besides Mack Cooper, it was Noah.

But she couldn't destroy his predictable world. He didn't deserve someone like her, always running from her past. Someone who still faced nightmares in the middle of the night.

And in the middle of some days.

No, Noah deserved better. She was not the settling-down type. Couldn't be. Not when she knew better than most how very dangerous the world was, how much complacency could get people killed.

And happily-ever-after? It was the worst kind of complacency. She loved the concept in books and movies, but it had no place in her real life.

"I'm going to make that call now to Sam, if you don't mind." Noah spoke up.

Erynn shrugged, sat behind her desk and started checking her email. "Sure, that's fine."

Erynn kept working at her desk and waited for his phone call to be over. When he finally hung up, she looked up at him, where he paced near the door of her office. "So?"

"He says he'll get a team together and get it done as soon as he can."

"Any time estimate?"

Noah shook his head and Erynn felt her heart sink, even though she should have known the answer. Nothing in this business came with a perfect timeline. It was foolish to expect this would. "He says he'll do the best he can."

"So what do we do now?"

"I guess, go on as normally as we can with the investigation—tugging the threads we have now, like the ME report, forensics at the crime scene and on the notes—until we've got another lead to follow. And look into Janie Davis and figure out where she's been for the past three years, what she's been up to."

Again Erynn felt a stab of pain in her chest, almost as if she'd been physically present for Janie's death. They hadn't been close. But they had been from the same place, had had enough of a past in common that there was a still a bond that had been violated. Like some distant relative you didn't like too much, but they were still family. And no one messed with family.

She snorted to herself. At least that was the way it was supposed to be. She'd had the bruises to prove that some people had believed otherwise until the state had finally taken her somewhere else.

That was supposed to be safer. But had anywhere in Erynn's life been truly safe?

She stole a glance at Noah, who stood near the door. Maybe that was part of the attraction to him. He was safety embodied in a Moose Haven police chief's uniform, his broad shoulders strong enough to carry the weight of the world and then some. His arms were solid, muscular from hours in the gym and in the woods, but what spoke of safety the most to Erynn was his eyes. They were dark hazel, like the woods at sunset, and when she looked at them she always knew someone was on her side.

Yes. With Noah she was safe.

However, it couldn't last. Nothing ever did. So, no, the safest course of action for her *heart* was to ignore his declaration. Stay friends, find some emotional distance while they worked this case together, day in and day out.

"Hey, I found something interesting."

Erynn looked up.

"Janie posted on her Twitter account yesterday, while she was in Moose Haven."

Not what she would have expected to hear.

"What did she say?" Erynn asked, already typing the address into the browser on her computer, like a lead couldn't appear before her fast enough. She couldn't even wait to hear Noah explain.

He didn't answer.

She looked over at him and he shook his head. "It's a short update. It just says, 'I'm finished running.'"

Was the obvious meaning the correct one in this case? Or was Erynn supposed to be digging deeper, finding some kind of message in there, one that wouldn't be apparent at first reading?

"Posted when?" she asked.

"An hour before she was killed."

Erynn's eyes narrowed. "So he was in Moose Haven, probably following her."

Noah nodded. "Yes."

How long? How long had he been in her town and, most important, was he still there?

She glanced to her right, at the blinds hanging from the small window that gave her a view of Moose Haven. She reached over and pulled the blinds down. No, they wouldn't stop a sniper's bullet, but right now, for her own sanity, she needed to know the killer couldn't see her.

When Janie had entered the office, Erynn had let herself believe that her feeling could have been from

Janie's scrutiny. But it was more likely that *he* had been watching.

Watching her movements, her daily habits, making notes of the weak points in her routine, when she'd be vulnerable to attack.

Erynn knew how this worked, had seen it before.

He watched. Watched. Watched. Waited.

Struck faster than a snake, left no survivors.

"What are you thinking?" Noah asked, his voice concerned.

What *was* she thinking? She was thinking they had to hurry. That it was too late anyway.

That she wished that, for once in her life, she could be free of her past.

SEVEN

Erynn had been distant all morning. It took a few hours for Noah to realize that she was not just putting space between them, was not distracted by the death of her friend.

She was scared.

She should be—he didn't blame her—because the man behind Janie's murder had been vicious and efficient. To have had this man haunting her for years... He didn't know how Erynn had stood up to it. But she couldn't much longer—that much was obvious from the strain around her eyes, the tightness of her lips.

She was holding it together, but only barely.

"Why don't I take you back to the police department with me, let you get a nap? I've got a cot in the closet in my office that I can pull out."

The look she gave him said everything she didn't want to say. She was resisting sleep. Maybe afraid of the possible nightmares?

"There are leads we can chase, but nothing so time sensitive it won't be there in the morning. You're exhausted, Erynn, and I think your time right now would be better spent resting. I doubt you slept last night and if we're going to sustain this pace..." He trailed off.

Still no reaction from her. She just stared. Blinked.

"You're just going to sit back and let this guy win, huh?" Noah hated to do it, to provoke her, but she needed to snap out of her daze. If poking her with a metaphorical stick would turn her back into the fighter he knew and loved, that's exactly what he'd do.

And it worked.

Erynn narrowed her eyes, turned to Noah. "Let him win? Sit back? Like I haven't been working toward this one goal for my entire life?"

She became a trooper because of this? It made sense, but he hadn't known. It felt like uncovering another layer of who Erynn was as a person. She was even more interesting than he'd always thought. This was something he wanted to know more about, hear more about, later.

"I didn't say you hadn't been working toward this," Noah said, "but at the moment you're just sitting there. We either need to dive into Janie Davis's background, or you need a nap so you have the energy to do that later."

"I need to stay here until the other trooper gets in later today. Or at least be reachable. So no napping."

"Maybe you should call your boss and explain. Make sure you've got some leeway in the hours you're on duty in case you can't sleep at night."

"While I'm on the phone with him, should I also tell him this case has a personal connection and just go ahead and get taken off of it?" Erynn shook her head. "Noah, this case is part of my life. It has been my entire life for years, wondering if it was going to start up again, waiting for another lead I could work in my spare time. If you care at all, understand that this is the most important thing in my life and I'm not going to jeopardize my involvement in it or give my superiors any reason to put me on leave from this job."

"Okay, I understand."

They spent the rest of the afternoon looking into Janie's background. Noah reviewed the old case files on the Foster Kid Killer, looking for information about the murderer and anything about his MO that could be helpful with this case.

By the time Erynn's shift at the station was up, he was exhausted and hungry and didn't know any more than he had that morning.

A glance at Erynn told him she felt the same.

"Want to come to my house for dinner?" He knew she probably wouldn't eat otherwise, and while they hadn't discussed where she should be spending the night and who would be watching out for her, Noah knew he had a vote. With him. He did not trust anyone else to do the job as well.

First he'd start with dinner. See if she'd listen to reason from there.

"Sure, dinner is fine." Her face brightened half a shade. "I'm starving."

"I'll drive us over in my car. I think my sister was supposed to leave your car there this morning."

Erynn nodded. "Sounds good."

They were on their way when Erynn started yawning.

"You're sure you don't need to get some rest?" Noah double-checked with Erynn. Okay, triple-checked.

Judging by the intensity of the glare on her face, maybe he'd quadruple-checked. There wasn't much he could do to make this easier for her. He certainly couldn't make it go away. So, somehow, besides solving the case, making sure she was rested and well-fed had become his highest priority.

"I'm fine, Noah. Still."

He hated the way she said his name, in that voice that was so familiar but standoffish. They had been through too much in the years they'd worked together for her to treat him like a stranger.

But that, he realized as he pulled into the drive of his house, was how she was treating him now. He hadn't realized anything could hurt quite so much.

"All right." He put the car in Park, turned to her. "I'll go inside, make sure it's all clear. Stay right behind me."

"You know I'm qualified to clear it myself, don't you?"

Was she scared or wasn't she? One minute she was staring like she might never recover from all this trauma. The next she was demanding he recognize that she was competent. Well, she was. He wasn't here to deny that at all, but it didn't take away his desire to protect her. To watch out for her.

He doubted she realized that, but if it came down to it, Noah would take a bullet meant for her to ensure that she lived.

Well, he loved her that much.

"I know you're qualified," he said instead of addressing the tension between them that he'd caused with his confession. "I never meant to imply that you weren't. But I want to clear it."

Had she heard more in his tone than in his words? Noah didn't know, but he knew that when she looked at him, he could almost feel sparks. He looked away. Knew staying focused was what was best for her.

"Fine. You clear it."

"You'll stay right behind me?"

"I will."

Noah climbed out of his car and headed for the front door. Darkness had come several hours before and the skies were clear tonight. But he wasn't looking around to admire the view in his corner of the woods. He was watching for any shadows that moved when they shouldn't, any sounds or signs that something was out of place, that something far darker than the Alaskan night was lurking in the blackness, waiting for Erynn.

He unlocked his front door, scanning the deck as he did so. It looked the same as it had; there were no eerie notes, nothing out of place. He did not have any reason to believe the man after her would be waiting there now, but then again, he didn't know when he'd strike. That was what instilled so much terror in Erynn. He'd read the files today for the murders the man had been responsible for. There was no predictable pattern for where victims were snatched, none for how they were killed. Serial killers commonly repeated their MOs, but apparently this guy felt like breaking the mold. His victims were foster kids, besides the one police officer, and he always left a note.

By the time Noah found another note, he had a feeling it would be too late. The fact that the killer had left one message warning them, getting their attention, was itself a deviation from his MO. Noah would need to figure out why that was.

He entered the house, locked the door behind them and moved toward the darkened rooms. Erynn did exactly as he'd asked and stayed right behind him. He was aware of her presence in a way he had been for as long as he remembered. Not just as a fellow law enforcement officer, but as *Erynn*.

"It's all clear."

"Is this the part where you feed me?" Her voice wasn't quite teasing but it was lighter than it had been earlier. From being in a safe place? Noah hoped so. That was the least he could give her.

"Yes. You need to stay in the living room, though, where I can see you at all times." Noah had never been so thankful for the open concept of the house, the way the kitchen island had a built-in range that faced the living room. He should be able to keep her in sight the entire time he cooked for them.

Erynn's expression wavered but she schooled her features quickly. Nodded.

Noah moved to the kitchen, watched as she settled on the couch. Closed her eyes.

There went the idea to carry on any kind of conversation.

Instead he focused his attention on cooking, making what he knew was one of Erynn's favorites: spaghetti. He threw some freezer rolls in the oven—he enjoyed cooking but baking wasn't his thing—and started some green beans sautéing in olive oil on the stove.

For half an hour or so he just cooked, looked at Erynn now and then. Either she was sleeping better than she'd expected or she didn't want to talk to him and was pretending exceptionally well.

When he'd finished cooking, he set the dishes and the meal on the table. "Erynn?"

She didn't stir. Apparently it had been genuine.

He walked to the couch, bent to the floor beside her. Her face was so relaxed, every trace of fear gone.

It seemed cruel to wake her. On the other hand, he had seen how she could be when she skipped meals. Whoever'd invented the term *hangry* had probably known Erynn.

He set a hand on her shoulder, feeling his heartbeat quicken. He squeezed his eyes shut and jerked his hand away like she'd burned him.

And maybe she had. Noah *had* to get hold of his emotions, had to keep his feelings for her separate from everything that was happening right now. Her safety depended on it.

If he kept making her feel awkward, if the tension between them didn't dissipate, he'd lose her friendship, lose the tiny bit of her he had. Noah didn't want that. So, for the sake of that, he had to put this to rest for now. Forget how he felt.

Or do his very best.

Noah squared his shoulders, took a breath and laid his hand on her shoulder again, reminding himself they were *friends*, just *friends*, and that was all they could be.

He shook her arm gently. "Erynn. Dinner's ready."

This time she stirred. He watched her eyelashes flutter as her eyes opened.

"Food's ready?" she asked as she blinked.

Had Noah ever noticed that her eyes weren't green as he'd thought for so long, but blue green, almost like the rivers near Moose Haven, the ones full of glacial silt?

Friends, Dawson. Friends.

He cleared his throat.

"Yeah. Food is ready."

"I can't believe I slept." She shook her head, sat up. Noah stood and walked back to the table.

"You needed it."

"I guess so."

They sat, ate with minimal conversation. Noah was thankful that things between them seemed more normal now. He didn't know if it was because Erynn had gotten some rest, which had taken a tiny bit of stress off, or if it was because he was making such a conscientious effort not to send any unwelcome signals. Either way, he was thankful and didn't want to risk it.

"Can I help you clean up?" she asked after dinner.

Noah shook his head. "I'd rather talk about the case some, if you don't mind."

Her eyebrows rose. "Did something happen when I was asleep? Did you learn anything?"

"Not yet." Though he was expecting a call from the crime lab in Anchorage anytime. The ME had transported the body there, since Moose Haven wasn't as equipped for an autopsy and all it entailed. If the Ice Maiden's fingerprints were in the system, they should be able to get an ID tonight. Then they could start looking into her background, working backward to find the trail of how she'd disappeared, maybe get some clues about who was behind it since Janie had implied the same killer was responsible for her death.

Was it really Michelle, the former foster kid who had warned Janie? Noah wanted to ask Erynn more about the woman, but not until the Ice Maiden's identity was more than speculation.

"So what did you want to talk about?" They settled back on the living room furniture, Erynn taking the couch and Noah a chair.

"I want to talk about Mack Cooper. There's very little in the files about his death."

He watched as Erynn's jaw tensed and the mask fell over her features again.

Had he ever realized how close to the vest she played things? He hadn't. Noah was almost sure of it. She was such an intriguing combination of open book and un-crackable code, but he hurt for her right now.

"There's not much there because the Anchorage Police Department didn't have any solid evidence that linked the serial killer to him."

"No note?" He had wondered that earlier when thinking through the killer's MO. It was another layer of confusion, something else about this killer that made him unpredictable and therefore more dangerous.

"No."

"No concrete evidence at all that indicated this serial killer was involved?" Noah didn't know how he was supposed to react.

"None."

He met her eyes. Waited.

"It's something I believe. I know other officers who did, as well. Several friends of my dad's who understood what the case meant to him and the lengths he would have gone through to have it solved."

He still didn't say anything.

"Seriously? You're doubting me?"

"No." He said the word slowly. And he knew how it sounded, but he meant it. He wasn't doubting her instinct, it was just another layer to process.

If her foster dad's death was linked to the other killings, as both she and Janie had believed it was… How? Why had he been killed?

Her dad likely hadn't been an initial target—it wasn't that he'd gotten close to the foster kids. It would, however, cement the idea that he'd gotten close to discovering the murderer's identity.

"Noah?"

"I want to see his case notes."

She was already shaking her head. "I don't have them."

His eyebrow quirked. Nothing he'd heard in the last five minutes sounded like solid evidence. He didn't say anything.

"You know what? I don't think I want to talk about this anymore tonight." Erynn had already stood. She moved to the door before Noah had a chance to wrap his mind around what she was doing.

"Listen, we can be done. Talk about it tomorrow."

"You know what, Noah? I don't think we can. Because if you can't believe me, believe in my dad one hundred percent, then I'm not sure to what degree I can work with you on this case."

"We have to work together. It's a case that affects both our jurisdictions."

"Oh, I'll share information. But I don't have to sit here in your house while you question me and the only family that ever cared about me."

She was out the door that fast, Noah scrambled to pull his boots on to follow.

Summer had driven Erynn's car to Noah's house as promised. Erynn must have had a spare key in her pocket because before Noah could tell her not to get in it, she was already in and reversing.

At least the car hadn't blown up. That was something to be thankful for.

He stood in the doorway for a second. Watched her drive away.

And then he grabbed his jacket, stepped outside, locked the door of his house and followed her.

Because that's what you did for the people you loved. Especially in the face of looming danger.

She'd overreacted. Erynn knew it as soon as she gunned the car's engine into Reverse and peeled out of Noah's gravel driveway. But there was no way to recover from that. She'd embarrassed herself enough around Noah today, and she hadn't been able to take his questioning her, or especially her dad.

He'd given his life trying to prevent Erynn from being hunted. Trying to prevent any of her friends and acquaintances in the foster care community from feeling that way.

He'd failed. And it stung. Badly.

She pushed the accelerator farther to the floor, tried to put Noah's face out of her mind. She'd go to the trooper station, sleep on the floor. Trooper Nichols was on duty and that would provide her with more security than her own home. No, she might want to get away from Noah, might not be able to take the way he pried into her past, but she wasn't stupid, didn't want to die.

She just needed some space.

The dark, winding road to Moose Haven from Noah's property outside of town stretched in front of her headlights. Snow had started falling and flakes hit her windshield rapidly.

The killer was out there somewhere, waiting. Erynn was afraid that if they didn't catch him quickly, one of these days he would finally get her, too.

Everyone else he'd come after was dead.

Maybe she should go back to Noah. He cared enough to keep her safe, she was sure of that much.

No, she'd be okay.

She kept driving, a little faster, whipping around curves at just the edges of the speed limit. Finally the lights of town were in view. She was almost there, almost safe.

Her phone buzzed. A text. She glanced at the armrest beside her. It was Noah. Where are you?

She glanced in her rearview mirror. There were headlights behind her, piercing the darkness she'd just driven through, illuminating the area even more brightly. Her shoulders relaxed slightly at the knowledge she was less alone.

The car edged closer.

Erynn frowned, slowed as she turned into the station parking lot.

The other car followed her into the lot.

Another glance in her rearview mirror gave her another view of the vehicle, this one better underneath the lights that lined the parking lot. Not Noah's car. Not one she recognized at all.

The person behind the wheel was unrecognizable—it was too dark to make out a face and Erynn thought he might have been wearing a mask.

Medium build. Likely male. Car was a four-door sedan. Dark colored. Traveling toward her at a high rate of speed, much higher than was safe.

She hit the gas, floored it out of the parking lot, the edges of her tires hitting the curb as she did so. Did she head farther into town, toward Miller's Point, despite knowing it was a dead end, or back toward the Seward Highway? The darkness and isolation would make it even more dangerous for her because no one would see if her attacker managed to hit her car, shoot at her, or anything else. But at least she'd have somewhere to drive.

Erynn glanced at her gas gauge. Plenty of gas. She'd take her chances with the highway. She whipped the wheel to the left, gunned the engine and grabbed her phone. Dialed 9-1-1.

"Moose Haven Police Department, what is your emergency?"

"It's Erynn Cooper. I'm being followed by a four-door sedan—last few model years. Unknown male driver. I think he's trying to hit me."

"Location?"

"I'm in town, heading toward the Seward Highway on Ballentine Street."

"We have an officer in your area. Stay on the line."

"Sure, but I'm putting the phone down." She wanted both hands for this. She turned down Seventh Avenue, toward Bear Mountain, then made a left almost immediately on Hamilton. The car followed her evasive maneuvers perfectly. Either the man following her was an expert stalker, a former race car driver or someone who'd been trained in defensive driving practices.

That was something she'd need to tell Noah so they could investigate fully later. She wouldn't let herself consider the possibility that she might not have that chance. She wasn't going to come this close to finding the man responsible for destroying so many lives and then let him get away with it.

The car edged closer as Erynn left the lights of town behind her. She passed the fire station. Passed the turnoff for Noah's house and Moose Haven Lodge.

Not much more in the way of civilization lay between there and where the Moose Haven turnoff connected to the Seward Highway. Only darkness and countless miles of Alaskan wilderness.

For a second she toyed with the idea of crashing her car on purpose, disappearing into the woods. Besides the fact that this was her personal vehicle and not her patrol car, and not one she could afford to replace, there was also her lack of wilderness skills to consider. She could probably last a little while in the woods, but she wasn't prepared for it. No, her chances were better in the car.

She gripped the wheel, her hands cramping at the pressure she'd been exerting since she'd realized she had a tail. She released them, one at a time, and flexed to get the blood flowing again. Who knew how much longer she'd be driving?

The road curved left and she hugged the bend even as she accelerated. Surely the person behind her had to tire of this kind of driving eventually. Unless, as she'd worried earlier, he was trained for it. It was a possibility Erynn hated to consider. Her dad had insisted he didn't think it was one of his fellow officers in blue. Erynn hated to consider the possibility, also. But her dad was dead and the killer was somehow evasive enough to have escaped capture. She'd be willing to suspect about anyone reasonable if it brought her closer to discovering the killer's identity.

The road ahead stretched in front of her and she could see all the way to the two-lane bridge over Moose Creek. Erynn wasn't sure if that was a liability or an asset at this point. Her pursuer was impossible to predict, but if she wanted to stay one step ahead of him, she had to try.

She sped up, but so did the car behind her, edging closer still. He increased his speed even more, to the point that Erynn wasn't comfortable driving any faster.

God, help me. She pressed the gas pedal another millimeter, as far as she dared, as the bridge drew closer.

She started over it, hands even tighter around the wheel. They were taking it too fast; bridges iced sooner in winter, and hadn't she made a career of public safety and done her best to keep people from harm in all areas? This was one of them. But she had to take the risk now. It was less dangerous than letting whoever was behind her catch up.

The front bumper of the sedan was so close now that she couldn't see its headlights. Erynn pushed her gas pedal a bit farther, but braced for impact in case it wasn't enough.

It wasn't.

Metal crunched on metal as her head slammed forward then back, though she'd done her best to hold herself steady. The back end of her car swung right. Because of the impact or as a result of the ice on the bridge, she wasn't sure, but she was slamming into the guardrail. Instead of another impact, she plowed straight into the rail without it catching her, and the car pitched right as the front nosed down, straight into the creek.

The water slowed the impact, but Erynn felt it shudder through her and cried out in pain as the seat belt caught her chest, sent a blinding flash of pain through her. Her screams were worthless, she knew; no one could hear her. Not right now. And not in a few minutes, when the man she'd been so desperately trying to avoid finally managed to catch up to her. The impact had shattered one of her windows and as the car sank deeper into the shallow creek, frigid water poured in, soaking her seats, her feet, climbing up her body and filling her with a cold so all encompassing, Erynn almost couldn't think. She struggled to put her thoughts together, keep some amount of coherency.

The officer in the area when she'd made the 9-1-1 call—had he gotten the message that she'd headed down the highway?

Please, God, if he kills me, don't let Noah find me.

She might not have been able to give him the answer he'd wanted when he'd made his confession, but it didn't mean she'd wanted him hurt.

No, Erynn admitted to herself as she saw a shadowy figure wade through the water as her vision blurred and threatened to take her under, she was fully, completely in love with Noah Dawson. Had been almost since the day she'd met him.

And would be until the day she died. Which was apparently today.

Erynn felt no fear, only resignation, disappointment, as the rising water in her car reached her shoulders. Her neck.

Then the dizziness and cold overtook her.

This was the end.

She'd tried.

And, just like her dad, she'd failed to succeed.

EIGHT

The water in the river was freezing and it burned Noah's legs, filled his boots as he trudged through it, fighting the current that pushed against his thighs, threatened to take him under.

He'd been too late, too slow. He'd hesitated when Erynn left and somehow in those short minutes a madman had managed to get on her tail and stay there, chasing her out of town and into *this*.

Noah had seen the crash, watched Erynn's car go over, and immediately driven close enough, jumped out and hurried into the water after her.

His gun was at his side, but he was exposed and vulnerable, and if the killer were armed, he'd be at a huge advantage. But none of that was worth thinking about now, because in Alaskan winter, the cold, swift-running water was as real a threat as any serial killer.

Noah stumbled, gasped against the shock of the cold water but kept moving. Erynn didn't have long.

He made it to her car, the open window adding to his panic when he saw the amount of water rushing in. Noah bent his head, could barely make out Erynn's shape in the darkness of the car. She was unconscious, her head back against the seat, and creek water was up to her neck. If her head fell in either direction, she'd breathe in water and her chances of survival would drastically diminish.

He had to get her out of there.

Noah ran his options through his mind as fast as he could. Go to the driver's side and break her window? Extracting her from the vehicle would be easier that way, but then he risked getting glass in her face. He didn't like that option.

Instead he broke a back window, desperate to equalize the pressure, and tried to pull the passenger door open. It gave easier than he'd expected and he wrestled it open all the way.

Thank You, God.

He moved his arms through the water, released her seat belt and then tugged her to him. She was entirely unconscious, as he'd feared, and unable to help him at all. Noah kept pulling till he finally had her in the passenger seat and then he yanked hard one more time.

She was in his arms and he was holding her tight against him, careful to keep her head near his shoulder, so that once they were away from the car he could stand, keep her out of the water and out of the danger of drowning.

As Noah moved away from the car, back into the middle of the creek, he looked around, searching the darkness for signs of Erynn's pursuer. The car had kept going when Erynn had gone off the bridge; Noah had seen that even as far back as he'd been, just edging into the straightaway.

Would the man come back or assume that the cold water and imminent hypothermia would finish the job he'd started?

Noah didn't know. His gun was soaked now, but would still work, though wrenching it from his holder would be more difficult now. He could defend them if necessary, but for how long? While guarding an unconscious Erynn?

He glanced at the road above, tried to assess the best route along the rocks that held the least amount of risk. Staying there, laying low, wasn't an option in these temperatures, not with how cold Erynn was already. Hypothermia was a danger here, even in the summer, especially if someone was wet. Now, in mid-December? It was edging ever closer to reality.

No, he needed to get her to his vehicle. He walked out of the creek, onto the rocks, praying his balance would hold even in waterlogged boots, and carried her to his car.

No signs of any other vehicles.

He opened the passenger door, slid Erynn into the seat, fighting back the panic at her stillness. He'd gotten there before the water had risen. Had she been breathing? Or had something happened to her in the impact?

She looked normal, just asleep. He hadn't felt anything amiss when he'd lifted her, but internal bleeding could be tricky.

Please, God, let her live.

The glaring white of the hospital floors, the walls, the ceiling, was giving Noah a headache. Tension in his jaw had crawled up to his temples and settled in not long after he'd arrived with Erynn and a flurry of activity had taken her away from him. He had counted at least five people, looking concerned, huddled around the stretcher they'd loaded her onto immediately. He'd been sitting on an uncomfortable green plastic chair for… He glanced at his watch.

Two hours. That couldn't be good.

Noah wanted to hit something.

"Noah Dawson?"

He jerked his head up, met the eyes of a nurse he didn't recognize. Waited.

"She's awake and asked for you." The nurse hesitated. "If you don't mind hurrying, she seemed to think it was urgent that you come with me."

Noah was already standing, walking to the double doors that led to wherever Erynn was. The nurse had hurried on ahead of him, taking him through the labyrinth of ER hallways. Finally she stopped in front of a door that was partially open.

Noah needed to get an officer posted here, in case he had to leave for any reason. Better yet, he needed to stay until Erynn was ready to be discharged and able to leave with him.

Still, the case needed attention. The scene at the bridge had to be processed. He wanted to be the one to do it, to be certain nothing was missed. But he didn't want to leave Erynn.

"She's a little beat-up," the nurse said, presumably by way of warning, as Noah walked through the door and pushed past the eighties-style patterned curtain.

Erynn lay in the bed, white sheet pulled up all the way to her chin, her face so pale the color of her skin was almost no different than the sheet, except for the bruises around her eyes. She must have hit something when the wreck happened and he hadn't noticed in the darkness and in the urgency to get her to the hospital.

Her hair was down, something he'd only rarely seen

since she always wore it up and pinned back while working and in a ponytail when off duty. It was thicker than he'd realized, the dark red falling in waves across her pillow.

She looked like she'd have quite the headache when she woke up. But she was beautiful, had never seemed more so to Noah. His stomach churned at the thought of the phone call he'd made while he'd waited. Any hint of partnership they'd had, any relationship, stood the chance of being destroyed because of the choice he'd made, but it was one he'd had to make. For her own good.

Her eyes blinked open. "You came."

"The nurse said you asked for me."

Erynn struggled to sit and Noah moved closer to the head of the bed to rearrange the pillows. "I did. I wanted to make sure you knew it wasn't an accident —the fact that I ended up in the creek."

"I know. I was following. Far enough back that who-ever was following you may or may not have noticed me, but I saw everything."

Erynn nodded, closed her eyes. Noah didn't know if he should say something or let her rest.

His decision was made for him a minute later when she opened her eyes again. "We need to get back to the scene."

"I need to get back, but I'm not sure you do."

"We have to investigate, see if he left any evidence." Her voice seemed to get stronger as her feelings about this case built and showed through her tone.

"Erynn…"

"Noah, I can't let him get away with this. Not again. Not anymore." She was shaking her head.

Noah steeled himself, took a breath. "I called your boss after I dropped you off."

She blinked, kept her eyes focused on his. "You…"

"Erynn, he needed to know why you weren't coming in today."

"And you get to be the one who decides if I'm fit to work?" The idea that redheads had a temper was a stereotype, Noah was well aware of that. However, this once it was true, when it came to Erynn. He'd borne the brunt of her frustration before—they'd disagreed and sparred over cases—but to his knowledge she'd never been truly angry with him.

Until now. Now, she left little doubt she was truly angry. Her tone was tight, her anger oozing out through her words, indicating she was on the very edge of control. Her facial muscles were tight, her cheeks red.

"You shouldn't have done that," she continued.

"I didn't have a choice." He felt his frustration bubbling, heard a tone coming out of his mouth that would have betrayed his feelings if he hadn't already done so. Had it really just been this morning? The day wouldn't end. "You could have died, Erynn."

"It's my job."

"No. This wasn't because of your job. This was because someone is after you, and no matter how much you want to be the one who solves this case, it's against protocol and you know it. You're too close, too involved and, frankly, it's too dangerous."

If steam could come out of people's ears, Noah would have sworn he saw it coming out of Erynn's.

"It wasn't your decision to make."

Noah shook his head. "It wasn't yours, either."

She stared him down. He hated her anger, hated that

it was upsetting her, judging by the rise in her heart rate on the monitor beside her hospital bed, and hated that it meant she was no longer officially involved in the investigation. But he stood by his choice.

When Erynn had been hurt badly enough that Noah didn't know when she could personally inform her boss? Yes, he'd taken it into his own hands. It had been what needed to be done.

"Leave, Noah."

He looked over at her, swallowing hard against the burning in his chest. He'd known she'd be upset. Had apparently underestimated to what degree.

"Erynn."

"I. Said. Leave." She punctuated the words, closed her eyes and turned away from him, pain chasing across her clenched facial muscles as she fought against who knew what kind of pain and to get away from him as much as she was able.

It hurt. More than anything he'd felt before. But Noah nodded, pulled the curtain behind him and stepped outside the door. Then he leaned against the wall, pulled out his phone. He wasn't leaving until he got someone else posted here to make sure Erynn would remain safe.

He wasn't going back in there, either. He knew when he wasn't wanted.

Pain stabbed Erynn's temples and her eyes and nose throbbed, a full symphony of facial pain.

It was amazing she'd escaped with as few injuries as she had. Especially when the last thing she remembered before losing consciousness was the water rising…

How had Noah gotten there in time? When he had,

how had he managed to pull her from the car by himself, fighting against the frigid water's current?

She had no idea. Did not want to think about it now. Because however heroic his actions, however much she'd *thought* he cared, he'd proved today that he hadn't. She'd devoted years of her life to this case and, from what he'd implied, was off of it within the span of... How long had she been out of it?

Erynn looked at the clock on the wall across from her bed. Hours. She'd been out for hours. Her head injuries must have been worse than she'd assumed. That explained the stabbing feelings and the throbbing.

In the space of a few hours, her purpose was gone. Over.

Now what was she supposed to do?

Erynn struggled to sit up further, pain in her rib cage making it harder. Not bad enough to be broken, but maybe bruised, she guessed.

She squeezed her eyes shut and fumbled for the phone on the bedside table. She assumed the hospital had never imagined it being used to conduct trooper business, but she wasn't a usual patient. She'd call her boss, do her best to smooth out whatever problems Noah had created.

It hurt to think he'd been the one to take this away from her. Especially after he'd claimed to care about her.

You'd think she'd be used to betrayal by those who professed to love her, especially after her childhood. But as it turned out, it never got easier.

Erynn punched in the phone number, waited for her boss to answer.

"This is Sergeant Dunlap."

"It's Trooper Cooper, sir."

"Cooper. I heard you were in a hospital, so why am I

hearing from you? I told the Moose Haven police chief that I'd send another trooper to cover for you at the station and assist the PD with the serial killer case, including this wreck you had tonight. All of it."

"It's not necessary, sir. My injuries aren't as...extensive as Chief Dawson may have led you to believe." Her heart still felt like it was suffocating when she said Noah's name, but at least referring to him as "Chief Dawson" gave her some emotional distance.

"He wasn't sure of your injuries. That's not why I'm sending someone. He mentioned a past you have with this case?"

Noah had been every bit as chatty as she'd hoped he hadn't been. As she'd dialed, she'd desperately hoped he had not told her boss everything, prayed she'd misunderstood.

But no. It was as bad as she'd feared.

"I don't have any kind of conflict of interest that could jeopardize my investigation, sir."

"I believe I'm the one who decides if something could jeopardize an investigation. Do you know how it will look to the prosecution if we get this guy, take him to court, and then one of the officers who worked the case knew his victims? Had attempts made on her life personally and potentially lost a family member to the same suspect?"

And now Erynn felt like she couldn't breathe. Not because of the bruises. Noah hadn't just told him most of it. He'd told him *everything*. Her dad wasn't officially a part of this case. Couldn't Noah at least have left that out? It was speculation Erynn was convinced was true, but it wasn't technically ethically necessary to have told her boss that—

"Listen, Cooper, I understand."

"You don't, sir." She cleared her throat, tried to back-track. "With all due respect."

"Okay, I don't. But I do know that you're angry. I know you're one of the best I have. And I also know we can't risk a case of this magnitude not holding up in court because of some technicality like you being too involved."

She had always known Sergeant Dunlap to be a fair man, and he still was, but his voice was like steel. No amount of talking was going to change his mind once it was made up. And Erynn was sure now, having heard him talk, that it was.

She was too late. She'd already lost the case.

Lost everything. All but her life, and that hung in the balance, as well. He'd killed so many of her friends.

Her head throbbed even worse, thrumming to the quickening beating of her heart. "So what now, medical leave? Are you transferring me?" Erynn wasn't sure what answers she wanted to hear anymore. Everything she'd cared about had already been taken from her. The entire reason she'd had this job...

"I want you to stay in Moose Haven for now and recover. And stay safe."

"If I'm not working currently, then my location is my choice, correct?"

"Yes, Trooper Cooper. But, as I'd like you to...informally assist, I would prefer you stayed there."

Her brow furrowed, she shifted the phone so it wouldn't press against her temple as she talked. "What does that mean?"

"I want you to rest and recover, but while you're doing so, you are still law enforcement, so anything about the case can be discussed with you. I believe your perspective, your insights, into how the man we are after works will be invaluable solving this case. I'd like you to work closely with Trooper Miller, who I'm sending down from Anchorage, and the Moose Haven PD, and make sure they know everything there is to know about the case."

That was more than she could have hoped for, given the circumstances. Erynn considered his words. "You want me to mentally work the case, but stay out of the way, and not be officially assigned to it."

"Exactly. We need to get this guy, Erynn. And I see why you want to be a part of it. But I can't have you officially working it…"

Erynn blew out a breath. "And you need me to work with N—Chief Dawson?"

"He cares about this case. I can hear in his voice it means almost as much to him as it does to you."

She swallowed hard, not sure what to think about that. If he cared, how could he have done this to her?

"I'll do my best to do what you want, sir."

"Cooper?"

"Yes, sir?"

"Mostly, I want you safe. You take care of that, all right?"

Erynn nodded. "I'll do my best."

They said their goodbyes and she set the phone back in the cradle on the table. The thing he was asking for, her safety, was the one thing she couldn't promise. Not even to herself.

NINE

Noah paced the hospital lobby, assessing his options. He'd assigned an officer to be outside Erynn's room. By all accounts, he should leave the hospital now, go back to the crash site and help the team there examine the vehicle as well as the guardrail for any evidence of tampering. It could be that the person after Erynn had put planning into what could also seem like a chance encounter.

He'd just started for the door when he heard a voice calling him.

It was James, the officer he'd posted on Erynn's temporary security detail.

"What's wrong?" Every sense on alert, no matter how sleep-deprived he was, Noah was ready to fight if Erynn was in trouble. If she was even more hurt because he'd listened to her and left...

He knew forgiving himself would be impossible.

"She's fine."

Officer James could have led with those words. Noah would have a talk with him later about that, when he was sure he'd calmed down enough to handle it professionally.

"Then what's wrong?"

"I think the hospital is planning to discharge her. I heard them say she has a minor concussion and some bruising. Possibly a cracked rib, but nothing that merits her staying for further observation. I wasn't sure where…" James cleared his throat. "I know you are… invested in Trooper Cooper's safety."

"I care about the safety of all the victims of crime in Moose Haven." Noah kept his face expressionless, but his officer raised his eyebrows anyway. So, yes, Noah had been right in his assumption that everyone in Moose Haven had been watching the two of them dance around their attraction for the past several years. "Cut to the chase, James."

"She wants to go home. I thought you told me she wasn't going to stay there because it wasn't safe, but she's an adult… I'm not sure what to tell her."

Noah should have known better than to think he could hand her off to someone else, like she was a responsibility to be delegated. She meant so much more than that to him. Always would, even if she never wanted to face that. Even if she left town and he was left trying to get over her.

She would never just be another person he knew, would certainly never be a victim of a crime that he'd helped keep safe.

He owed it to her not to leave her now, just because she was upset.

"Tell you what, Officer James. I can take over for you here if you can go down to the site of the accident and see if they need an extra hand."

The other man was already nodding, his eyes wide. He was a relatively new officer on the Moose Haven force, the youngest by far. Now that Noah thought about it, he didn't tend to give him as many interesting assignments as the more experienced officers. But if he didn't, how was he going to learn?

Noah patted him on the shoulder as he walked past, feeling every one of his thirty-one years. He pushed through the doors back to the hospital hallway and almost ran right into Erynn.

"What are you doing here?"

Her voice did not sound angry, just surprised. Maybe…chagrined? Or was he hoping for that? She was wearing a pair of green scrubs and Noah could only hope she'd borrowed them from a nurse upon her discharge from the hospital rather than stolen them to try to make an escape.

"Hoping I wouldn't catch you leaving?" He tried to keep his voice steady, raised his eyebrows even, to try for a casual look.

It was easier than admitting how much the sight of her in that hospital bed had shaken him, how thankful he was that she was up and about now. Even if she was angry with him for the decisions he'd made.

Erynn looked down at her clothes. "I borrowed these from a nurse. Seemed like a better option than leaving the hospital in doubled gowns."

Noah was pretty sure she'd have fought someone before she'd let herself be put through that kind of humiliation.

"Should you be leaving already?"

"You sound doubtful, but I'd like to point out that you aren't my doctor."

"No, but did he give you permission to leave?"

She stopped walking and looked up at him, her face

void of any humor. "I asked you to leave and you didn't. And now you're giving me a hard time."

"Answer the question, Erynn."

"Yes. I can leave. I'm supposed to take it easy."

She wouldn't, and they both knew it, but at least she'd answered. He stepped aside so she could pass, then walked behind her to the door. "Any particular place you're headed?" He tried to ask it without sounding sarcastic, but the way she'd been treating him still stung enough that it was hard to shake off.

Her shoulders sank. She stopped walking again. Noah waited, thinking she'd continue any minute, but she didn't. Instead her shoulders started to shake.

On alert again, Noah moved past her, looked down at her face to see what was wrong. "Are you hurting?" Her eyes were squeezed shut; her cheeks looked hollow. Hopeless.

She shook her head.

"Nothing hurts?"

She looked up at him, her eyes shiny with unshed tears. In the years he'd known her, he'd never seen Erynn cry. And they had worked a few cases together that could have shaken the calm of just about anybody.

"I don't know what to do, okay? I told you to leave and you didn't. I'm not surprised, because you never listen." She sniffed. "But I want to get out of here and I don't know where to go. My house isn't safe. I have no real friends who know who I am, really…" She trailed off again.

Noah already had an arm around her, pulling her closer to him as they continued down the hallway.

"Come on, we'll go to my house and talk there about what's next." The killer knew where it was, but he'd proven he could track Erynn anywhere. Noah would much prefer any confrontations happen on his turf. Having her there was a calculated risk, but one he felt good about.

She nodded, might have said, "Okay." It was hard to tell with all the sniffling. He stopped in the lobby of the hospital, made sure he didn't see the slightest sign of anything out of place outside, and then walked her to his car. Once they were inside, he drove to his house, the only location he could think to take her.

"You're sure this is okay?" Her voice was soft, vulnerable.

"It's safe."

"That's not what I mean."

He met her eyes. She'd stopped crying but she looked like she was emotionally spent, and it broke his heart.

"I mean is it okay with you if I'm here? I've not exactly been the best friend the last couple of days."

Not for the first time, Noah regretted his words to her earlier, when he'd told her how he felt. He'd pressured her, exactly what he shouldn't have done when she had so much to deal with, and he hated knowing he was making her life more difficult. "You're fine."

"I'm serious, Noah." Her voice was stronger now. Resolute.

Noah didn't know what to say. So he didn't. He just drove in silence till he finally reached his home, pulled up in front of it again. And prayed as he did so that he'd know how to handle Erynn's exhaustion and stress. Because he wanted to take it away from her, something he knew he couldn't do. But he could at least *not* make things worse for her, which was what he needed wisdom to do.

* * *

If she'd ever felt this much like a shell of herself before, it was in the days after her adoptive dad had been killed. She still remembered walking around, knowing people were going on with their lives and that her world had been shattered. She'd continued living with her adoptive mom, but nothing had been the same after that. Erynn felt almost worse now because she had no optimism to help give her hope, no real expectation that they would bring the man responsible for terrorizing her to justice. Instead she just had a heavy knowledge that she'd almost become another of his victims tonight. And that she hadn't done anything to prevent it, at least not before the danger started. If Noah hadn't showed up… Erynn didn't know how she was going to keep driving over that creek without the past threatening to drown her.

Noah didn't say anything as he led her inside. She could feel his tension, though, and wished she knew if it was from the case itself or from the weirdness between them. She wished they could go back, before Noah had mentioned anything about his feelings and wondered about hers. What had been so wrong with the past few years of dancing around the issue?

But it was too late now, she knew that, and they had no choice but to find a way to move forward. As friends. Because much as she might want to, Erynn could offer him no more than that, couldn't take the risk that being part of a family would involve. That would mean you'd be gutted inside if something happened to someone in your family, meant that you were walking around all day with your heart outside of your body. She couldn't do that to herself, either, not with as much as her dad's death had hurt. And she'd only known him for a couple of years.

Erynn's heart couldn't take any more loss. She had told herself for years that she hadn't let anyone close because of her job, because it made sense for her to maintain a certain amount of distance as a law enforcement officer. But maybe she'd been fooling herself. Or trying, anyway.

"I've got updates on the case," Noah told her once he finished checking the house, presumably for bad guys. For half a second she debated staying quiet, not begging him to tell her anything he knew, but she couldn't.

"What did you find out?"

"The identity of the Ice Maiden."

Erynn's inhale was sharp. She'd assumed when Janie had been the one to go missing that the Ice Maiden case was connected to the Foster Kid Killer. And up until Janie had walked into her office, she'd thought Janie was dead. This opened up another line of questions. Had a random woman been victimized to make it look like Janie had been killed? Or…

"Her name was Madison Reynolds."

Erynn swallowed hard, closed her eyes and put her head between her legs.

Another person she'd known in high school, someone who had lost the only family she'd had because of their poor choices and gone into the foster system. And now she was dead.

Had been for three years. *Three years* and no one had reported her missing, at least not that Erynn had heard. She'd tried to keep tabs on anyone she had known in the foster care system, because of the danger they'd been in. But life was busy, her job...

Were those just excuses?

It was unconscionable that a person had died and for three years no one had missed her.

Erynn did not want that to become her. Could not let it.

But knew it would.

"But Michelle...?"

"Died in a car crash last year."

"Suspicious circumstances?" Erynn wondered aloud.

"Nothing the Kenai police noted. We may never know if it was truly an accident."

"I need to go to sleep." Those were the words that came out of her mouth, the only ones she could force through her lips. She was the furthest thing from tired, but she needed space. Needed Noah not to watch her every expression. Needed to keep them from getting any closer.

Because if she fell apart out here, he'd hold her, comfort her, make her feel like maybe it could be okay.

She couldn't let him do that. But she wasn't sure she had the strength not to let him. She stood.

"Erynn."

His deep voice made her think of Moose Haven, of the mountains that surrounded the town, tucking it in against the water like something from a Hallmark movie. It made her think of home. Whatever that was.

Whoever that was.

She swallowed hard against the lump of grief building in her throat.

"Did you know her?"

A tear escaped her eye, slipped past her lashes and down across her cheek. Followed by a second. A third.

She nodded.

"Come here."

He was on the couch, holding out his arms to her, and Erynn didn't even try to stop herself. She sat on the couch, leaving hardly any space between her and Noah, and let him pull her to him, wrap an arm around her. Her head fit so well into the spot between his shoulder and his neck.

Unlike the way she'd leaked tears at the hospital earlier, Erynn really let herself cry now.

For Madison. Janie. Matt. William. Sydney.

For the lives they could have lived.

For her dad.

For her future and the ways she wished it could be different.

Erynn didn't know when she finally stopped. All she knew was that the sobs kept coming, but less frequently and, with every one, Noah didn't flinch, he just held her closer.

She fell asleep, sitting up on the couch, next to the man she knew she had always loved but who she could never tell.

Whoever said that things would look better in the morning had never had a serial killer after him, Erynn decided. The bruises across her shoulder and chest, which came from the seat belt, had left a deep ache and she still had a slight headache. She was on her second cup of coffee, brewed by Noah while she'd been sleeping on the couch. And nothing looked any different.

She stole a look at the kitchen, where Noah was

cooking them breakfast. Over the first cup of coffee, he'd told her his plan for the day, which involved following the trail Madison had left up until her death. Noah told her that while she'd been asleep last night he'd discovered Madison's credit card had been last used in Seward, not far from Moose Haven, a few days before she'd been killed.

Today they were going to go to Seward to see if there was still any trail to follow three years after Madison's death. Erynn didn't want to get her hopes up. Seward was a tourist hub in the summer, with cruise ships often docking and swelling the town's growth to many times its usual size. The chances that someone would remember Madison weren't huge. Unless, of course, she had given them a reason to remember her. Had she had any suspicion that her life was in danger?

During the Foster Kid Killer's reign of terror, over a span of two years, no foster kid in Anchorage seemed safe. Even though police had suspected the killer was targeting a group with more in common than being foster kids, they hadn't quite been able to narrow it down.

Now that Erynn knew for sure her dad's concerns about her being in danger had been well-founded and that Janie and Madison had also become targets... perhaps that would make finding him more doable.

Wait, hadn't the killer said she was the last one he was after? Erynn frowned. "Noah, that note that was left on your porch the other day. What exactly did it say again?"

His face wrinkled into a frown. How could he still be so handsome, even with an expression like that? He must not have shaved this morning, because even from here she could see the stubble lining his jaw. It seemed appropriate for Noah. Mostly clean-cut, but with rough edges, enough of an adventure-seeking personality to keep life interesting.

"'She's mine. You're next. And then it's over.' Something like that." He looked back at breakfast then at Erynn again. "Why?"

"Just thinking." That implied he'd killed everyone else he'd intended to. Surely she'd be able to find another link between them all now. And if she could figure out who'd had enough access to them to decide he wanted them all dead...

Then they'd have the killer's identity and it would just be a hunt to find him.

Of course, if this trip to Seward turned up any information, that would also help.

Noah set a plate down in front of her. "You need to eat."

"Bossy this morning, aren't we?" The teasing words flew from her mouth before she could stop them. She was close to apologizing when she noticed Noah was smiling. Maybe that was because they were back to their regular banter. That would make her feel relieved... So instead she said nothing, just ate the food like he'd told her to.

The last time she'd been this hungry was...? Days ago. Apparently her crying last night had cleansed some part of her that had been holding stress inside and had given her just a bit more preparedness to face today.

"Did you call the Seward police to tell them we're coming?"

Noah shook his head. "Not yet. At this point it would be pointless to let them know. Nothing indicates that the crime took place there for sure. We just know she was in Seward. If we need to loop them in, we will." He glanced in her direction. Looked back at the road. Then looked at her again.

"What, Noah?"

"So, did you talk to the troopers yesterday?"

There was a bit of reality she'd been trying to put off dealing with as long as she could. Sometimes, denial was such a nice place to live.

"I did."

"And?"

She shifted in her seat to face him. "I think it's probably what you expected. I'm off the case, not working currently. I'm supposed to lay low, stay safe." Like it was that easy. On either count.

"You're welcome to tag along with me anywhere I go."

"That's what my boss suggested. You weren't the one to give him that idea?"

Noah shook his head.

Neither of them said anything for a minute before Noah spoke again. "Do you realize yet that neither of us was against you? That this was the right thing to do?"

She did, but that didn't mean she had to like or admit it.

"Yes, I do." On second thought, better to say the truth aloud. There was enough between the two of them already. She didn't need to add to it by holding a grudge.

"Thanks, Erynn."

They ate the rest of the meal in silence. "Ready to go?" Noah finally asked.

"Yes."

Erynn started toward the door, Noah close behind her. He said nothing until they were in the car and buckled in. After he'd turned the key, he looked at her. "Listen, Erynn…"

She waited, felt herself holding her breath almost unconsciously. Surely he wasn't going to elaborate on their earlier, one-sided conversation.

"I think you know him."

Her heart pounded in her chest, but for a different reason than she'd anticipated. "The killer?" She didn't know why she asked. She knew what he meant.

"Yes. After we're done in Seward today, I'd like to sit down with you and compile a list of suspects, people we should be looking at, anything like that."

She nodded. "Okay."

Wading deeper into her past with Noah was enough to make her want to crawl in a hole and hide until everything was over. Not because it was so difficult to face, but because she didn't want Noah to think of her this way. She wanted him to see her as strong, capable.

But if anything had the capacity to break her, it was this case, her past.

And he'd have a front-row seat to the fallout.

TEN

Noah did not know for sure that they were being followed on their trip to Seward, but he'd started to feel uncomfortable as soon as he'd left his driveway. Erynn didn't seem to have noticed anything, and since she couldn't do anything to help even if she knew he was concerned, he hadn't said anything to her.

Something she would yell at him for later, Noah was fairly certain.

For now she was sitting in the passenger seat with a notebook and pen she'd pulled out of his glove box, writing something down. He assumed it was the list he'd told her he wanted to work on later.

She'd asked about the words left on the note, seemed to think they'd carried some significance. Because the killer said she was the last one? Or because it gave her a hint as to who could be behind this?

Noah tightened his grip on the wheel, glanced in the rearview mirror again. Still no sign of any cars too many times in a row, no one driving too close. He was being paranoid; that had to be it.

It was different, working a normal case compared to trying to keep a friend safe and knowing there was someone close who wanted her dead. He'd have never guessed at the amount of pressure. He might owe all his siblings an apology for keeping so calm when they'd been in similar situations with the ones they loved. At the time he'd thought he was being the steady one. The oldest. Now he just wondered if he hadn't realized how it felt to care this much about someone who wasn't family.

Yet.

He swallowed hard against the thought. He had no right to consider the idea of being a family with Erynn anytime, but especially not now. When he'd made his ill-timed confession, she'd said they'd talk later, but Noah could tell by the way she'd acted since then that it wasn't the best idea to put too much hope in that. She didn't want him to be part of her life the way he wanted her to be part of his. He loved her enough to accept that.

"So what's your plan when we get to Seward? Just walk to the different places we know she visited and see if anyone can help us?"

"That's the plan at the moment." Noah was still deciding if it was foolish for Erynn to be out in the open that long. And did she really feel physically capable or were her injuries from last night worse than she'd let on? He could only trust her assertion that she was fine physically. And he would be with her, wasn't planning to let her out of his sight. And they needed to have boots on the ground for this kind of work, read people's facial expressions when they saw the picture of Madison he planned to show them. Asking questions over the phone wouldn't give the same kind of results. And Noah hadn't wanted to come without Erynn.

"Something's wrong, isn't it?"

He kept driving, glanced over at her.

"You're unusually quiet, Noah. I'm upset by everything but I'm not stupid. Is someone following us?"

He admired the way she kept her voice calm, even after all she'd been through the last time someone had followed her. He couldn't keep his suspicions from her anymore.

Noah nodded.

"Do you know who?"

"No. I don't see anything out of the ordinary. Just a bad feeling."

"I trust your bad feelings."

Her voice was sweet, gentle. And, yes, trusting. He'd worked hard at this job for years, determined to be the kind of man people could rely on. But no one's dependence upon him had ever meant as much to him as Erynn's.

He wanted to deserve it. Did not want to let her down.

"Still, Erynn, there's no reason to worry."

"There's a man out there who wants me dead. I think that's plenty of reason to be at least mildly worried."

He couldn't argue with that.

They drove the rest of the way to Seward in silence and, before long, Noah was pulling his car into the parking lot across from the Sea Breeze Inn and Restaurant. The credit card charges he'd found for Madison hadn't been time-stamped, so all he had was a list of places they needed to visit.

"Keep your guard up, okay?" he said to Erynn after coming around to her side of the car to open her door. He had his duty weapon at his side, as did Erynn, but guns weren't a guarantee of safety. Their first defense was good situational awareness. They were across from the Seward harbor, an open expanse of docks and boats just in front of and below them. The shops in this part of town were lined up on the other side of the street, adjacent to the parking lot.

"I will pay attention but I'm not sure what good it will do if you haven't seen anything." There it was again, that faith in him that Noah wasn't sure he deserved but desperately wanted to be worthy of.

Noah put his arm around Erynn, his hand resting on her upper arm, and pulled her closer to him. She looked up at him, eyes a little wider than usual.

"Easier to keep you safe if there's less space between us." Noah smiled a little. "But if you'd rather just walk next to me that's fine."

If anything, she moved closer, and they walked in sync to the restaurant and through the front door.

The waitress approached them. "How many?"

Noah was already reaching into his pocket for his badge. "Hi, I'm Chief Noah Dawson from the Moose Haven Police Department. I wanted to ask someone a couple of questions about a customer you had."

"Sure, when? I've got to warn you, a lot of people come through here."

Noah glanced at Erynn, whose face already looked half a second from wincing at the unlikeliness of this panning out.

"Three years ago."

The waitress shook her head. "I didn't work here then, I'm sorry. Would you like a table, though? Anything to eat? We serve breakfast for another hour."

"No, thanks, we've already eaten. Is there someone who worked here back then that we could talk to?"

The waitress shrugged. "Maybe? I'm not sure. I'll go ask." She disappeared behind the swinging kitchen door.

"Not feeling like we're going to make a lot of progress here," Erynn whispered as they stood there. Some of the diners had started looking at them and beside him he felt Erynn shift, her discomfort evident.

"We need to stay and see what she says."

She didn't argue, but when Noah looked at her he wasn't sure she agreed. The waitress came back out almost immediately. She was shaking her head. "The chef is on his way out to talk to you. He's the only one who was here three years ago."

"If these people's breakfasts are delayed, I'm pretty sure some of them are going to riot," Erynn mumbled.

The door swung open. "I'm Manny." The burly man looked like he had enjoyed quite a few dishes of his own cooking, Noah noted, but his face was open enough. If he was made nervous by their presence, he didn't show it.

"I understand you worked here three years ago."

Several people walked through the front door just then and had to make their way around Noah and Erynn, stepping between them and Manny.

"Is there somewhere we could go to talk?" Noah asked. He was eager for their investigation, which they wanted to keep low-key, not to be the center of attention in this diner anymore.

Manny shrugged. "I can't have you in the kitchen. Insurance reasons. Too many fire hazards, you could cough on my food, make someone sick. It's a bad idea all around. Just ask me what you need to ask me."

"Do you remember ever seeing this woman?" Noah

pulled the picture of Madison from his pocket and watched Manny's face as he studied it, but the man gave nothing away.

Manny shook his head. "I'm sorry. I don't see many of the customers since I'm in the back cooking, but since I'm the only one who was here, I wanted to come see if I could help you."

"She doesn't look familiar?"

Again he shook his head. "I'm sorry, but no."

"Does this place have security footage?" Erynn gestured toward a camera in the corner.

The man laughed. "It's fake. My son put it there to deter people, but no, no actual footage."

Disappointment sunk like a rock in Noah's stomach.

"Thanks for your time." Noah put the picture back in his pocket.

"I hope you find something." The man disappeared back behind the double doors.

Erynn sighed. "I'd hoped maybe we would find out more than I thought we would."

"Eh, there are always dead ends. Maybe we'll get all of ours out of the way early and find someone soon who remembers Madison, recognizes her at least."

"Where to next?" Erynn asked, pushing the door open as they walked and stepping onto the sidewalk.

Noah glanced at the car and debated walking to their next stop.

"Let's get back in the car." It didn't take him long to decide. It kept Erynn safer and that was his top priority. Though solving this case was, too, obviously, since he couldn't keep her safe in the long term until they had the man who wanted her dead behind bars.

They drove to the next place he wanted to check out: a local bookstore.

"Welcome to Between the Lines." A woman's voice greeted them and Noah turned to see who had spoken. The proprietor was probably midsixties, her white hair cut close to her head. Her expression was warm, welcoming.

"I think she'll help us," Erynn whispered.

He did not know why she had the same feeling he did, but it was a good sign. Hopefully.

"Hi, ma'am. I'm looking for a woman I think may have shopped here, purchased something?" He kept the police part quiet for now since it hadn't made much of an impact on how his investigation at the restaurant had gone and he truly did want to keep their search low-key.

"Well, depending on who you are, I may be able to help." The woman's voice was friendly enough but Noah thought he saw a hint of something in her eyes. She knew more than she was letting on. She had to, for the very mention of him looking for someone to catch her attention and put her on guard to such a degree.

"It's a woman who shopped here three years ago." He waited for her to react, but she just kept watching him. "I have her picture." Noah slid it out of his pocket.

The woman glanced down at it then looked back up at Noah. "And who are you?"

He pulled his badge and ID from his pocket again. "Chief Noah Dawson, Moose Haven Police."

The woman's shoulders sagged and she started to cry. "Something happened to her, didn't it? I've wondered for three years, hoped that maybe she was wrong…"

Wrong about what? Noah wanted to ask, but they needed to start at the beginning.

"She was killed." Erynn spoke up.

"Are you from the Moose Haven Police Department, also?"

Erynn shook her head. "No, Alaska State Troopers."

Noah glanced at her, shook his head. Tried to remind her that this was his case now, and he needed to be the one asking the questions. For her own safety, for the integrity of the case should it ever come to prosecution, he needed her to stay quiet.

"Ma'am, I'd really like to talk to you about this woman's disappearance." Noah glanced around at the empty store. As far as he could tell, they were alone. "Is now a good time?"

She moved from behind the counter, already heading for the front door, where she reached for the Open sign, flipped it to Closed. "Yes. I would like to talk about it now."

"First, what's your name, ma'am?"

"Sabrina Baxter."

"Thank you, ma'am. I just want to make sure I know your name so I can be back in touch with you if I have more questions after our talk today. So, you remember this woman from three years ago. Can you tell me why?"

Sabrina nodded. "She was upset when she came in here, asked me to keep an eye out, and if anyone followed her, to call the police. I did watch her the entire time she was in here, and saw her leave. She went from here toward town. She mentioned she was heading to Exit Glacier to meet someone. But I don't know who. And I don't know if she was followed."

Her tears picked up again. "I'd hoped when I didn't hear anything about anyone being attacked or something like that, that she was okay."

"And when was this?"

"April, three years ago."

It lined up with the Ice Maiden's assumed time of death, which was difficult to pinpoint when a body was discovered in a frozen state. Based on the amount of snow on the body, it likely hadn't been there long before they'd discovered it in May three years ago. At least that was one part of the case they'd gotten right.

"Did she say who she was worried might be following her?" Noah asked.

The woman shook her head. "Not a word. Just asked me to call the police if I saw anything. She bought a stack of books—a rather odd selection."

"Are you able to look up receipts that far back? Because we'd love to know what they were."

"I still remember. It was such an odd combination. She bought a book about home decorating and two about private investigators. Not fiction—nonfiction sort of how-to books that explained the profession." Sabrina moved back behind the counter, opened one of the drawers and pulled out a pad of paper. "I can write the names down for you."

Noah glanced at Erynn. She looked like she was struggling with her emotions. Fear? Or survivor's guilt?

"I'd appreciate it," he said to Sabrina.

She finished writing, handed him the slip of paper.

"Did she stay here in the store long?"

The woman was already shaking her head. "No. Just long enough to buy those books. And then she was gone." She brushed a tear from her cheek.

Erynn felt her own eyes welling up with tears in response to the emotion Sabrina Baxter was showing. How terrible for her, to know she might well have been one of the last people to have seen Madison Reynolds alive. She wished there was a way to reassure the woman. It wasn't like the bookstore owner could have called the police without a credible reason to do so.

"Do you have an idea about who was after—?" Sabrina started to ask.

"Madison." Erynn supplied her name despite Noah's earlier look reminding her that this wasn't her case anymore, that she was supposed to be quiet. She was trying, but it was only possible to a point.

"I'm assuming since you're here and it's three years later that she...that someone..."

"She was killed, yes." Erynn didn't sugarcoat it, didn't see how she could. She set her hand on the counter, leaned forward a little bit toward Sabrina. "But you telling us anything you remember may help us—" she shot a glance at Noah "—may help Chief Dawson figure out who was behind it and bring him to justice."

Sabrina nodded. "I've told you most of what I remember."

"Anything else? Time of day, the weather?" Noah asked.

The woman nodded. "Yes...it was morning, I believe, and I know it was raining that day because I remember noticing when the woman left that she'd tracked mud all through the store. It wasn't bad to clean up, but I do remember doing it after I watched her leave."

She looked at Noah. "Do I need to be concerned since I've told you all this? Will whoever was responsible come after me?"

Erynn doubted it. The serial killer hadn't hurt any bystanders that they knew of, hadn't murdered anyone besides foster kids, with the exception of her adoptive dad, and he'd been a lot closer relation.

Noah shook his head. "No, you'll be okay. I'll stop at the local police department before I leave town to fill them in and make sure they have a basic awareness of what we are dealing with. Just as a precaution."

Sabrina nodded, sniffed again and wiped her eyes. "Thanks for coming in. I'll make sure to call you if I have any questions. Do you have a card?"

Noah gave her one and then put his hand on Erynn's back to guide her out of the shop. They'd only made it a few steps from the door when she shook her head. "I feel bad for that woman."

"Because she's the last one to have seen Madison, as far as we know?" Noah turned his head toward her when he asked the question. Erynn blinked. His face was so close to hers. She could tell by his widened eyes and the way he backed up that he'd been closer than he'd meant to be. Somehow it was nice to know she was not the only one caught off guard. Her heart might have skipped a beat or two, her eyes noticed his lips, the way the stubble from his goatee begged her to reach out and touch it...

Erynn looked away.

"Erynn?"

Oh, right. She'd forgotten the conversation they had been having, the question Noah had asked. "Yes. And I feel bad because she seems like she feels guilty."

"Because she knows more than she said?"

"No. Because she wishes she could have done more." Erynn knew what that felt like. All too well.

"There's nothing she could have done." He set a hand on her arm and she looked up. "You, either, Erynn. There's nothing you could have done for any of them."

Any of them was a phrase that echoed, ricocheted like a gunshot in her soul. So many people had been lost to this person's madness. In her heart she knew he was right. She couldn't have saved them...at least most of them. But she could work as hard as she could now to bring whomever it was to justice.

If she hadn't been taken off the case.

"Where next?" Erynn asked to focus on the positive, keep herself from getting too discouraged.

"She also spent money at Jack's Souvenir Shop." Noah gestured ahead of them to a building set apart from others.

"Think we'll get as lucky there as we did at the bookstore?"

"I doubt it. But we may as well try."

It was close enough that they walked. It had not been lost on Erynn that Noah had chosen to drive from the restaurant to the bookstore. Her guess was that he hadn't wanted her exposed for that long, something she appreciated. But not driving from here to Jack's, when it was so close, made more sense.

If she had to be taken off a case, especially one that meant as much to her as this one, Noah was the man she wanted in her place. He'd never let her down. Not once.

And whatever else was true, Erynn knew that she could trust him.

"You doing okay?" he asked.

She nodded, not wanting to share any more of her thoughts with him right now.

He had to know she felt something for him, at least admiration. She'd been on his side in more than one arena of life, supported his investigations above and beyond the call of "interagency cooperation" duty. He knew how she felt. Right? Yet he'd told her they didn't have to talk about it until the case was over.

What if she changed her mind and wanted to talk about it before then? Erynn stole a glance at him. He didn't notice; he was too busy scanning their surroundings for threats, making sure she stayed safe, even now, when her mind had wandered away from the case and onto something she really didn't have the luxury to be considering right now.

Still. She wanted to talk. Maybe.

Was that crazy? Could they possibly have some kind of future…?

"Erynn, get down!"

Noah's shoulder slammed against her and she felt his weight pushing her down at the same time she heard a gunshot. Pain exploded as she fell on her wrist and Erynn wanted to lift her head, look around and figure out where the threat was, but Noah was on top of her, shielding her with his body.

Willing to die so she wouldn't have to.

Just like her dad.

A sob choked Erynn's throat but she was powerless to move. "Where is he?"

"On top of one of the buildings."

Another shot, this one close enough that the broken sidewalk sprayed pieces of concrete in her direction, hitting her on the arm.

"We've got to move. You can't get shot because of me." He just couldn't.

She felt him shift his weight.

"Okay, Erynn, see the bushes to the right?"

"Yes."

"If we can get behind those…"

He didn't have to count, tell her to get ready or anything. They had known each other long enough, Erynn guessed, that their minds were so in sync that they moved as one toward cover.

When they were behind the bushes, he grabbed her arm. "We need to run."

"To the car?"

"Yes."

They did, Noah running behind Erynn.

Once they arrived, he stayed behind her as she got into her seat, shut the door behind her and then ran to his side. They peeled out of the parking lot and only then did Erynn almost start to breathe again.

He'd almost gotten killed. Because of her. Grief pressed in, suffocated her with its weight. To think she'd been close to thinking maybe she and Noah *should* talk about what they'd avoided discussing or confronting for so many years. She couldn't now. Couldn't ever.

"Get your phone out. Call the Seward Police Department. I need to focus on watching our surroundings."

Erynn nodded, pulled her phone out with shaking hands.

"Nine-one-one, what's your emergency?"

"Someone is shooting on Second Avenue."

"We've gotten a few calls about it, but thanks for letting us know. An officer is on the way." The phone clicked.

Erynn panicked. "Wait! No! This is different. They were shooting at me!" But the operator had already hung up.

Erynn looked at Noah. "Do I call back or call the police department's main number?"

She could see him weighing their options. She knew

him well enough to know how he preferred to work. If it was just his safety to think about, he'd make the report in person. She was slowing him down. Was she hindering progress on the case?

"Call the police department."

"We can go by if you want to."

Noah shook his head. "I'm taking you back to Moose Haven. Now."

She wasn't about to argue. Not now that the adrenaline was finally fading. Her hands had stopped shaking but her insides felt like they were trembling. She had been that close to the person who had killed her dad. Had come heartbreakingly close to being killed herself.

She wanted to go home.

"Erynn."

She looked up at him.

"Call, please."

She'd gotten distracted. She looked the number up, dialed and asked to speak to an officer.

"I'm Trooper Erynn Cooper." She figured introducing herself by her title was still accurate and legitimate even though she wasn't acting in her capacity as an officer. "And I was shot at on Second Avenue just now."

"Do you know the identity of the shooter? We have officers on their way to the scene. Are you there now?"

"No, we aren't." She glanced at Noah. "I'm with Chief Noah Dawson from the Moose Haven Police Department. We are headed back to Moose Haven."

"We'd like to talk to you in person, if that's possible."

"Hold on just a second. Sorry." Erynn muted the call, looked at Noah. "He wants to talk to me in person. What, am I just going to tell him no?"

"Tell them they can come talk to me in Moose Haven

if they want, but you aren't leaving the car. I don't want you out in the open when we know this guy is right here, running loose."

"Would it be possible for you to meet us at the Moose Haven Police Department? We're in a bit of a hurry to get out of town."

"Yes. I'll head that way now."

"Thanks." Erynn hung up the phone. Shook her head. "That's got to be an unusual request for them, but he said yes, so that's good."

"Good."

"Did the killer know we would be here?" Erynn asked as she stared out the front window of the car, trying to make sense of what had happened.

"I don't see how he could have."

But it was possible, even if neither one of them wanted to say it. Was he tracking their movements? Erynn would make sure to ask Noah to check the car for tags.

Or, possibly even more terrifying, was he just watching *her*?

She shivered. Wondered if she would ever be free of this nightmare. And prayed for its end, which couldn't come soon enough.

ELEVEN

"And you have no idea of the identity of this person?" asked the Seward police officer. Noah had called the officer, whom he'd met before, to meet them at his house, for Erynn's safety. Officer Jake Williams was about Noah's age, a man with a thick, Southern accent who'd moved up from Alabama several years before. They had had several conversations about Alabama football last fall when working a case together about an accidental death on the Seward highway.

"That's correct," Noah confirmed. "But we're working it from several angles."

Officer Williams seemed to be considering it. "And the Ice Maiden case…the victim was found on the Harding Icefield, correct? Closer to Seward or Moose Haven?"

"Moose Haven."

"Where had she been living?" the other man asked.

"Anchorage, I believe." Noah looked to Erynn, who nodded. He hated that she was more familiar with the victims than he was, promised himself he'd go over all the files online tonight to make sure he knew them at least as well as she did. It was the least he could do after having her taken off the case as a result of a phone call he'd made.

"I'd look into that some more. The killer isn't likely from around here, so find some of the connections the victim had in Anchorage that the others had."

"That's our plan for tonight." Erynn spoke up.

Noah hadn't realized, had thought she might be tired enough she'd want to sleep early, but a quick look at her face confirmed that she was in focus mode. He'd be willing to bet she wouldn't top five hours of sleep a night until this was over. Erynn was determined at this point, and when she got that look in her eyes, few things could stop her.

It made him scared for her and proud all at one time.

The woman made him feel more than he'd ever imagined he could. Like his world had been black-and-white and she'd exploded color into it.

He didn't want to lose her. Not to this madman, not to anything else.

"Keep me posted if you can." Officer Williams stood. "And I'll check on Sabrina Baxter, like you asked."

"Thanks, we appreciate it." Noah rose and walked him to the door. He locked it behind the other man once he'd left and walked back to the kitchen, where he found Erynn in the kitchen mixing chocolate syrup into a tall glass of milk.

"Hitting the hard stuff tonight, I see." He smiled.

"I've learned about two former friends' deaths in the last twenty-four hours, had someone shoot at me and the man…and my…and at you. I'm pretty sure I've earned every ounce of this chocolate milk."

Noah tried not to let his mind catch on her hesitant description of him, tried not to wonder what it meant.

"You have, no doubt. So you told Officer Williams we're working on Anchorage questions tonight?"

She nodded. "I thought maybe we could work out some angles, figure out who we need to talk to, and then drive to Anchorage tomorrow."

"Absolutely not." He didn't even have to take the time to consider that. He'd taken Erynn with him to Seward and look what had happened. Other officers were working this case; he'd had a phone call earlier to make sure they were all on the same page and to talk about the progress they'd made. If benching himself for a couple days, doing nothing but making sure Erynn had constant protection was what he needed to do to keep her safe, it was well worth it to him.

"It needs to be done, Noah." She didn't even look up from where she was still stirring. He walked over to her, caught the startled expression on her face when she saw him standing there in front of her. He took a deep breath, needing more courage for moments like this than he'd needed for when they'd been shot at, and put his hands on her upper arms. He looked down at her, straight into her eyes. "It doesn't need to be done by you, Erynn. I won't—I *can't* let anything happen to you."

"Noah." She looked away but did not make any move to pull out of his arms.

He stepped closer.

"I thought I'd lost you today, Erynn." He reached up, brushed a strand of hair from her face that must have fallen from her ponytail when she was mixing the chocolate milk. "I have no idea how I could make it through something like that, so I'm not going to let it happen."

"And that means—" was it his imagination or was her voice a little more breathless than usual? "—that you can't let me out of the house? That I'm going to stay here until this is all solved, wrapped up neat and tidy with a bow?"

In his experience, cases this important never wrapped up neat and tidy. He could count the number of bows he'd seen in his career on one hand.

"No. But it does mean I'm not going to let you take unnecessary risks. There are plenty of files you could go over."

"Noah..."

He was closer now than he'd ever been to her. Could see the sky blue flecks glinting like diamonds in her eyes. Noticed for the first time that her nose had the lightest dusting of freckles on it.

Noticed not for the first time that she had the most kissable lips he'd ever seen.

"Noah." Erynn tried again. "I don't want you hurt because of me. And what you said... I know that we... that there's something here, okay? I won't deny that. We're both adults and you can handle the truth."

What was between them wasn't one-sided. He swallowed hard, his heart thudding in his chest as his stomach jumped with the first bit of hope he'd felt in a long time.

Noah took a breath, spoke slowly. "Since we're both adults, don't you think that rather than try to protect me from getting hurt because of you, you should let me make my own decisions?" He kept his voice low, dropped it almost to a whisper at the end, because staring into her eyes—without her flinching, without her looking away or making excuses as to why they shouldn't be together—for this length of time was robbing him of his ability to talk.

"What you said earlier..."

"Today?" He didn't want to misunderstand, didn't dare to hope she was having the conversation he'd told her they would put off until later.

"Yesterday. At the glacier."

"Yes?" Noah waited, wondered if he was finally going to hear his words echoed back to him. Instead she looked up at him, met his eyes for a few more seconds that stretched out in a way that made him breathless. Then she tipped her chin up, leaned forward and closed her eyes, her thick lashes fluttering.

His eyes shut subconsciously seconds before her lips met his. She'd initiated the kiss and he let her lead. Her lips were soft at first and he met them with equal softness, building in intensity only as she did, his lips exploring hers like he'd wanted to do for so long.

She was the woman for him. *God, please let this work.*

She continued the kiss long enough that Noah wanted to keep going, wanted it desperately, actually, but he loved her enough to pull back. Feelings. Passion. It had all built between them for years and he wanted to make sure he stopped long before it became difficult to do so.

He loved her too much to mess this up. Didn't want to betray her trust, not in any way.

Even as he pulled back, he wrapped his arms around her and folded her against him, her head tucking against his chest. "Erynn…"

"Shh. Don't say anything. Not yet."

So he didn't. He just stood and held her and pretended this could last forever.

Erynn didn't know if she was most surprised it had taken so long for the two of them to kiss, or that Noah had been the one to end it, or that she'd started it in the first place. Badly, too, like she had a right to Noah's kisses, to his lips and his love.

She knew better. But she didn't want to admit it to herself right now. For these five minutes, she wanted to know what her life might have been like if she'd not been the target of a killer, if she hadn't learned early and so thoroughly how painful it was to lose the people you loved.

Maybe that was why she hadn't been able to say the words back to him. He'd wanted to hear them, she'd seen it on his face, knew his expressions as well as her own, to the point she sometimes felt she could read his mind. But instead of saying them back, she'd kissed him. Maybe that would be enough, would help him understand he wasn't alone in his feelings, when she couldn't give him the same assurance.

Might never be able to.

For now, standing there, listening to his heartbeat, against the solid reassurance of his chest, had to be enough. And it was.

"Erynn."

She looked up at him, waiting for him to ask for the conversation she knew she couldn't have yet. Instead she met his eyes, warm and brown and filled with a look she'd used to dream of seeing in a man's eyes one day. He reached out his hand, cupped her jaw and tilted her face up to meet his again.

This kiss she'd started, he finished with nothing short of perfection. Had she realized kissing Noah would be *this*…whatever it was? Erynn had lived a lot of life, had adventures, taken chances, but she wasn't sure she'd ever felt as alive as she did right now, ignoring the world around them and kissing the man she loved.

Erynn blinked at her own unedited thoughts, stepped back.

Avoiding saying the words to Noah wouldn't do her any good if she was having the feelings anyway. The goal was supposed to be to avoid the emotions altogether, to build a wall around her heart to keep it safe, keep everyone safe.

She shook her head. "You know we can't…"

"I don't know anything like that, Erynn Cooper. You keep acting like it's impossible, but I know you, and you know me better than anyone else does. I've seen us work together over the years. I've seen how you care about people. I watched you in church. You love Jesus, Erynn. I love that about you, and I think…I think you love me, too."

From anyone else the words could have sounded arrogant, but from Noah's lips, in the reassuringly gentle firmness of his tone, Erynn knew they were not arrogant. He was only stating what he believed to be true.

And he wasn't wrong.

God, help me. You know why I can't do this, can't feel this way. Take it away, please.

"The case. Can we finish the case first?"

She was stalling; she knew it and was fairly sure from watching his expression shift that Noah did, too. But he nodded, always a gentleman, never pushing.

It made her want to kiss him again, grab his jacket lapels and kiss him and kiss him until she couldn't remember what she was so afraid of anymore.

But loss, fear, they would always find her. Hadn't this week reminded her of that?

"I need you to let me go to Anchorage."

He shook his head. "Not after today. You need to be here."

She opened her mouth to argue. He touched a hand to her mouth, his fingers brushing her lips like another kind of kiss. The way it made her mouth tingle with loss had her forgetting all arguments. *Focus on tonight. One step at a time*, she reminded herself. Eventually she'd get to Anchorage. For now she needed to focus on rebuilding some emotional walls and on making a list of who they needed to investigate, both suspects and potential witnesses that could have been overlooked.

"Let's work on the case, okay?" Noah cleared his throat. "As friends…if that's what you want."

Erynn nodded. "Friends."

If friends could be so conscious of the other person's nearness… Could be aware of the broadness of another's shoulders… Could imagine what it would be like to be able to step across the line without having to jump backward across it again…

He took a breath and let it out slowly. "Can we make a couple lists? Try to make sense of this?"

"I think that's a good idea." Erynn forced her mind to focus on the task at hand. She'd tried thinking through lists earlier in the day, but seeing them written down always helped her.

Noah had left her standing in the living room and walked to the adjoining study—to get paper for himself, she guessed—so she settled down on one end of the couch. Noah would hopefully interpret her unspoken signal and take the other end, keeping the notepad between them.

Something, anything, some physical reminder that they had to stay apart. Physically, emotionally.

He walked back in and she felt his presence to her toes.

Yeah, because space between them could possibly fix the chasm she was drowning in.

"Got it." He smiled at her.

She reached for it, started writing the list of victims so far, her hand shaking a little as she wrote "Mack Cooper."

Noah settled in on the couch. Directly next to her, her knee almost touching his thigh. She reminded herself to stay focused, took slow breaths to try to convince the beating of her heart to match that rhythm.

"Okay, also." Noah held out a hand for the notepad. "May I?"

Erynn nodded.

He tore the first page off, with the names she'd written, and set it on the coffee table in front of them. "We also have ways they're connected. So list those. I'll write, you think out loud. Go."

"We were all foster kids, except my dad."

"He's a close enough connection I'm comfortable saying he was an anomaly. What about his MO? Was everyone killed by a gunshot like Janie?"

Erynn shook her head. "No similarities in the way people died. Which is strange for a serial killer, though not unheard of."

Noah nodded. "Okay, what else?"

"We all lived in Anchorage at one time."

"Do you mean that some of the people were foster kids in other cities and towns or that they moved away after high school, those who…lived that long?"

"The first. One of the victims had moved to Kenai, but when that family was in Anchorage for a grocery shopping trip, she disappeared and was found later, dead."

"So the killer is likely based in Anchorage. And everyone was killed there initially…"

"Well, until recently. The last two murders were both down here, either in Seward or Moose Haven."

"He followed people when they were on vacation? Or he moved?"

Erynn shook her head. "I'm not sure." Something had gotten stuck in her brain, but she couldn't quite work out what it was. Something had "pinged," caught her attention. If she could just wrap her mind around it.

But sleep deprivation, stress, adrenaline, made it impossible. She felt her face wrinkle into a frown.

"Hey." Noah's hand on her arm did nothing to untangle the knots of confusion in her brain. "We'll figure it out."

"You honestly think that?" She never asked people that, didn't like being let down when they made promises they couldn't keep. Nevertheless, she trusted Noah.

"I do."

She had to swallow hard, look away from his eyes, which made her want to dive deep into the land of what-if and out of the reality she knew was true to her life. She couldn't kiss him again. Should not have done it the first time.

Or the second.

"Is there a chance people stopped going to Anchorage? Did the foster kids he had been after start avoiding the city, so his preferred targets weren't accessible?" Noah asked, tapping a pencil on the table.

"You mean that's why he stopped killing them there?"

Noah shrugged. "There's a chance, just an idea."

They'd done this with cases before, thrown around ideas, saw what stuck. It had produced results more times than she could count. Maybe he was right. Maybe they really would be able to solve this one, too.

"Or he has a job that makes him travel?"

"Could be."

"Or it's different people committed the first group of murders and then these two, Janie and Madison."

Erynn stopped. Certain details, like the notes, hadn't been made available to anyone outside of law enforcement to preserve the integrity of the investigation and to stop copycats. But what if there were two killers and the first had…died? Or had somehow gotten someone to help?

She didn't know if any of that made sense, either.

As much as she hated to admit it, nothing would—not until she had some sleep.

"I can't do this anymore tonight, Noah. I'm sorry. I'm exhausted and nothing is making sense anymore." She looked away as she said the last words. She'd meant them about the case. Hadn't she? Still, she prayed he wouldn't read anything else into them, wouldn't see the way he'd managed to chip away at her armor until she was just a woman who wanted to have the freedom to be in love with a man who loved her back.

God, if that wasn't going to be an option for me, if You knew my heart couldn't take it, all this loss, all these risks, why give me feelings for him?

"Sleep."

She stood and so did he. He reached for her and she knew if he tried to kiss her, she wouldn't be strong enough to resist. She'd lose herself in the feeling of his lips on hers, again and again, as long as he wanted her.

Instead he wrapped her in his arms, in a tight hug that filled up the empty spaces inside her heart. Had her blinking back tears. He was the best man she'd ever met.

Worth loving.

Maybe.

"Sleep well," he said and released her.

She walked to the bedroom, changed into pajamas and then opened the door so he could see if anyone tried to climb into the house through her window. She got into bed, closed her eyes and let sleep take her.

TWELVE

Two days. Forty-eight full hours had passed since they'd been shot at in Seward, and Erynn was going stir-crazy. Noah hadn't let her leave his house. And, yes, she was an adult, made her own decisions. But she also trusted him and if he thought she needed to hole up for a bit…

Well, she might as well. She'd gone through the files Noah had brought her, and while every word had reminded her of the past, none of it was new information to her or useful in her investigation. What else did she have to do?

Noah was a different story. She'd noticed his restlessness yesterday as the day had stretched out and they'd done their best to toss around ideas of things to investigate. He had passed the better ones along to his colleagues at the Moose Haven Police Department and the troopers. But she could see what it was doing to him to be benched.

She could feel it. After all, she felt the same.

However, she didn't have a choice. He did.

"We really need to talk, Noah."

His head snapped up. She realized her mistake

quickly and clarified, "About the case. And us both being stuck here."

"I'm not taking you out anywhere investigating. You've been fine for two days, and he hasn't even tried anything, which tells me this is the best place for you right now."

Erynn wasn't sure. Her uneasiness was growing with every hour that passed, not diminishing. But Noah didn't need to know about any of that, did he? It wasn't like she was keeping a specific threat to her safety from him. He knew why she would be worried, on edge. But her feelings now were probably just out of control. Erynn didn't need to tell him, not until she had a reason to believe she was in more danger than they already knew she was in. She had another point to this conversation.

"I think you need to go back to work. In person. Not delegating from here."

He shook his head. "I'm not leaving you and just hoping for the best, Erynn."

He wouldn't have done that for a single other person they'd helped protect over the years. Erynn knew it, appreciated it. But it needed to stop. They were stalled and if they didn't make some traction on the case soon, she was worried it would go cold again.

Until a moment when she let her guard down and then it would be too late for her, too.

Noah must have read the expression on her face because he sighed, sat in a chair across the living room from her. "Tell me what you had in mind."

"I will stay here. I can see that's important to you and I'm not stupid enough to risk my safety or the case by taking unnecessary chances."

"Not like a few days ago when you left the safety of my sister and Clay's house and headed to the glacier?"

"Exactly. Not like that." She had been wrong to do that. Might not feel like admitting it to him, but she was woman enough to admit it to herself. "I will stay here. Get another officer posted here. But we need you out there, solving this. You care about it. You're motivated to see it through, more than anyone else but me, I think."

And she couldn't work it. Did not have a choice. It didn't stop her from spending her days bent over a notepad, trying, but she knew that to be making a real impact she needed to be out there, as well. Not that it mattered. Her orders from her boss had been clear, and she knew Noah was right about it being too dangerous for her to be active in fieldwork right now, even unofficially.

"You'll stay here."

He was actually considering it—something she hadn't counted on.

"Yes." Erynn nodded.

"Let me think about it."

Three hours later they were finishing up lunch when Noah looked up at her and sighed. "Okay, we will try it. For this afternoon. And if I don't like how it goes… If you feel more uncomfortable than usual…"

"Then you can come back to house arrest with me." Erynn shrugged. Sure, she was uneasy already, so it would be difficult for her to feel less so. She sure wasn't going to say anything to risk Noah agreeing with her idea. Because she knew in her heart if they didn't change something, didn't get more aggressive, the killer was going to slip through their fingers.

Again.

"Thank you."

It felt strange. Surreal—maybe that was the word her mind was grasping for—to watch him go through the motions of getting ready for his day to hunt the murderer.

"Any ideas which leads you're going to follow up on there in the outside world?" She tried to keep her tone light as she watched him lace up his boots.

"I've been in contact with some of the officers in Anchorage who were active during the case's beginning."

She hadn't braced herself for that answer. Her dad's colleagues? "Any progress?" she asked, hoping she kept her voice casual but doubting she had.

"Not sure yet." He stood, walked to the closet near his front door and pulled out his jacket. "I'm still waiting to hear from one guy."

The chances it was her dad's former partner were looking pretty good. She had tried to talk to the man, when she'd grown up and become law enforcement, but he hadn't offered her any leads. Had just told her that he knew her dad wouldn't have wanted her risking her life going after the same man he'd been trying to bring to justice. Erynn had believed him. Mostly. But she still felt like he knew more than he was saying, and wished she knew what it was.

Maybe he would tell Noah.

She nodded, not sure what she should say, how much to hold close to herself. Did Noah realize how often she did that? She wasn't like his sisters. Well, at least one of them. Kate tended to keep quiet most of the time; she was introverted. On the other hand, Summer sometimes seemed to think by talking. Did he know that the times Erynn was quiet were the times she was pondering things the deepest?

"Let me know if you can."

He reached for the door. Stopped, looked back at her.

She got goose bumps down to her toes at the warmth in his look. She'd had too little of that in her life.

"You're sure this is okay with you? The troopers had an extra man, Trooper Pederson, and he's going to stay here with you."

Erynn hadn't met him, but maybe that was better. It would be awkward if someone she usually worked with were acting as a kind of bodyguard. Except for Noah. Somehow when he was protecting her it seemed natural. Right.

"It's fine, Noah."

He stepped toward her, pressed a kiss to her cheek. "I'll be back in a few hours. At any point if you feel like this isn't working or you have a bad feeling, I don't care how unfounded it is, you call me and I will come back, okay?" His eyes were serious, the corners around them crinkling with worry.

"Okay. But I'll be fine." She could only hope that would be true. She knew that letting Noah go was what was best for the case. So, in the grand scheme, best for her.

And then he was gone, a tall, blond man entering in his place. "Hello." She nodded a welcome to Trooper Pederson then went back to the living room. She'd find a book to read and maybe make those few hours go by a little faster.

The book hadn't helped. Neither had the TV show she'd turned on to try to distract herself. Erynn finally busied herself cleaning. In the few positive memories she had of her birth mother, she remembered her cleaning a lot. So somehow it was a thing she could do that seemed to help the world feel right when it would otherwise have felt all wrong.

She started with the floors in Noah's house, though they weren't too dirty to start with. She'd noticed early on in their friendship that Noah was no slob, so it didn't surprise her that he kept his home relatively clean, though she couldn't say she'd ever been there before this week.

Their friendship had been close but casual. She'd kept it that way on purpose, avoiding spending time together at either of their houses or really alone anywhere. Had known they needed to keep space between them to keep her from admitting she'd fallen for him. Or vice versa. A lot of good that had done, because once she was really in trouble, Noah had been the first one she'd called: the man she trusted to help get her out of it.

Apparently you could only hold people at a distance and pretend for so long. Erynn scrubbed harder.

Once the floors were even cleaner than they had been, Erynn moved from there to the windows. As she dusted one of the front windowsills, she noticed that Noah's front porch was covered in mud people had tracked up. It had dried and turned to dirt. There was a broom right next to the door.

Erynn looked at the front door and glanced back at the trooper, who was sitting at Noah's dining room table.

"Mind if I head outside for a few minutes?"

He was already standing. "I'll have to come with you. My assignment was pretty clear."

She had expected that, though it didn't make it any easier to know that she was basically being babysat 24/7. Instead of being upset, she nodded. "That's fine."

While he grabbed his jacket, Erynn grabbed hers, noting the pile of extra winter gear Noah had by the door. She hadn't brought a hat or gloves. Borrow some of his or just go without? It wasn't as if she'd be outside for long. But she took them anyway, pulled them on and figured at least this way she wouldn't be cold while she was sweeping.

The cold air made her feel more awake, more alive, as soon as she opened the door. Maybe being outside had been what she needed the entire time. Trooper Pederson was in the front yard, no more than maybe ten feet away. She knew Noah would not allow even that distance between them if he was here with her, so maybe she'd mention the idea of going outside more often to him when he got back tonight. He'd feel better if he was the one out there with her, but she was really benefiting from the fresh air.

"Erynn?"

She didn't like the apprehension in the other man's tone. "Yes?"

"Could you head inside? I thought I saw something in the woods I'd like to check out."

"Yep, I can do that."

"You're a trooper. Did I understand that right?" he asked.

"I am."

"Do you have your weapon?"

"I do," she said.

"Get it out and wait for me inside. Lock the door. I have a key."

She did not waste any time dropping the broom where she stood—Noah would understand—and hurried back inside the front door to her comfortable prison, praying it would be enough to keep her safe this time.

A minute passed. Nothing. She glanced out the window. Paced the living room. Decided that wasn't helping and moved to sit in a chair at the table. Had it just been a few hours ago that she'd sat there with Noah and they'd come up with the plan for him to get back into the case, to leave her there? She was questioning it now.

He'd said to call if she felt uneasy at all. Now counted, didn't it?

Two minutes passed. She would give Pederson three more minutes. Then she'd call Noah, lock herself in a bathroom and wait for him to arrive.

She heard the back door ease open behind her and released the breath she'd been holding.

"Did you find anything?" Erynn shifted her weight in the chair where she was sitting, turned to look at Trooper Pederson.

She saw a flash of black, saw work pants, and looked up, alarm racing through her at the thought that this might not be Pederson after all.

Pain exploded in her head as something hard connected with it. Her pulse thundered in her ears, each beat like another blow.

And then she felt nothing.

Unease prickled the back of Noah's neck, down his back and shoulder blades as he backed his car out of his spot at the police department to head for his house. He'd not been able to get nearly as much done as he'd hoped to, because Erynn had never been far from his mind.

The ME had determined that the cause of death for Janie Davis was indeed a result of the gunshot wound to the heart. It had been what they'd assumed, but having it confirmed was good. Madison Reynolds had died of blunt force trauma to the head.

The best part of his day, though, had been the message waiting for him on his work phone. Erynn's dad's former partner at the Anchorage Police Department, retired Officer Danny Howard, had called back. The man was retired now, it seemed, but, yes, he had information he thought could help. It had been all Noah could do not to plan a trip to Anchorage for tonight, picking up Erynn on the way. But things had been quiet for a few days and, as long as she seemed relatively safe in Moose Haven, he had no plans to change the status quo. Better not to take the risk.

He'd call Danny Howard when he was with Erynn. That was a conversation she'd likely want to be present for.

He glanced down at his phone on the armrest. No new texts from Erynn. He'd probably driven her crazy earlier today, checking in as often as he had. The same with Trooper Pederson, though the man had been gracious.

At least now he was on his way back, didn't have to trust her safety to anyone else until tomorrow. *If* he decided to go through with this plan to go to Anchorage.

The closer he came to his house, the more the knot of dread in his stomach kept growing. Noah looked down again at the phone. He could call her now, hear her voice and know she was all right. Sure, she'd laugh at him for his overprotectiveness, but it would be worth it for his peace of mind.

He picked up the phone, hit her speed dial number.

It rang. And rang. Went to voice mail.

Noah frowned. Tried again. He was probably three minutes away now. Three minutes and he could see her face-to-face, laugh about the fact that she'd accidentally left her phone somewhere, and lecture her about not doing that, lest she take years off his life by making him worry.

It kept ringing. Voice mail again.

One more minute of driving. He slipped his phone into his pocket as he pulled into his driveway, relief flooding him to see that nothing was out of place. Trooper Pederson's car was where he'd left it.

Except…what was that in the yard?

Noah slammed the gearshift into Park and left the car without shutting the engine off, a sick feeling in his stomach as he ran to the prone figure. Yes, he'd known what the killer was capable of, but he still hadn't imagined Erynn could really be…

The crumpled body in dark clothing was too large to be Erynn.

Trooper Pederson. Noah rolled the man onto his back, felt for a pulse and found one, and immediately pulled his phone out and called for backup. He looked around the yard, didn't see any signs that the threat was still present, and ran across the yard toward the house. She could be okay. She could have locked herself in a closet, could have shot an intruder, for that matter. None of what he'd found so far meant she had to be dead.

His heart was pounding in his chest. "Erynn!" Her name exploded from his lips.

The front door was locked. Another bit of reassurance. He fumbled in his pocket for his house key, thankfully on a different ring than his car key, which was still in the ignition.

Unlocked. He stepped inside.

The back door stood wide open.

"Erynn!" he yelled again, not hearing anything that would indicate she was still inside. He ran to the back door, his eyes catching on a slip of paper.

Same cream paper. Same handwriting. Probably the same pen.

I've got her. The end.

He could put his fist through a wall. Instead he left the note where it was, knowing he'd ball it up and compromise evidence if he so much as touched it, and ran to his car.

Erynn was out there somewhere. Backup could handle the scene at his house; he'd call to let them know that she was gone. But Noah wasn't going to trust her safety to anyone else from now on. Not that he blamed Trooper Pederson. The man had probably done his job the best he could, but he wasn't a man in love.

Noah was. And he needed the woman he loved to be okay.

THIRTEEN

Throbbing, thundering pain in her head was the first thing Erynn noticed. Was she awake? Asleep? She tried to pry her eyes open but couldn't. She was so tired… No she couldn't sleep; she had to figure out where she was now, where she'd been. She remembered Noah's house. The person inside who wasn't Trooper Pederson. Being hit hard over the head.

He had her.

He sat in front of her, in the driver's seat. Slight build. All in black. A mask on his head and a heavy black jacket on.

Nothing about him would help her identify him.

Erynn almost couldn't breathe. She fought to give her lungs the air they needed, even as she tried again to open her eyes, this time succeeding. She was in a moving car's back seat. She didn't dare move her head and give away that she'd come to, but she could see through her peripheral vision that the woods were passing by at about a normal speed. Good, he hadn't moved from dangerous to reckless yet, was still trying to avoid detection. That might give her the tiniest sliver of hope.

Hope. A word she hadn't had much use for most of her life. But maybe…if she lived…

Goose bumps crept down her spine, across her shoulders. She was in a car being driven by a serial killer who had watched her friends take their last breaths. Had stolen part of her forever family from her. It was too much to process, too overwhelming for her mind to try to wrap itself around.

If she was going to live, Erynn had to get out of the car. She knew that much from her training.

She moved her arm slightly. No seat belt. Which made sense since he likely wasn't too worried about her dying in a car crash.

Why had he moved her at all? Why not just kill her where she was, right there in Noah's home? Unless, of course, it had turned into a game for him now. They hadn't yet established a motive for any of the foster kid killings, but Erynn had evaded him before, had remained alive for many years. That could explain the change in pattern.

Whatever the reason, his intent was still clear. There wasn't even the slightest possibility he would let her live. She *needed* to get out of this car. Could looking out the window again give her a hint as to where she was? Erynn squinted. No, only trees. There was no way to tell how long she'd been unconscious. They could be minutes from Moose Haven or most of the way to Anchorage. Or he could have taken her down the Sterling Highway toward Anchor Point and Homer, where more miles of untamed wilderness would provide the perfect place for him to hide her body.

Erynn wasn't going to let that happen. She looked at the door handle. The car looked like a Ford, judging by the finishes, a newer model like Clay drove. His doors unlocked automatically from the inside when you pulled against them; Summer had told her about how her dog could open the doors from the inside, even when the car was locked.

Since there was no way to surreptitiously unlock the door before trying to make her escape, Erynn was going to have to hope that worked in this vehicle.

If this was one of the highways, which was what it looked like, there were no stop signs along this road, nowhere that a driver would have to slow down enough to make what she was about to do less than foolish. Erynn made up her mind to stay still until he slowed down for a curve. She'd try it and see what happened.

It was a morbid game to play, but if asked if she'd rather die at the hands of a madman or because she'd broken her body by accident trying to escape? She'd take the second option every time.

Her chance came only a few minutes later. She felt the car ease off the gas, then a more intense deceleration as he pushed the break.

Erynn grabbed the handle.

"Hey!" He hit the brake harder and she took her chance, launching herself from the car and doing her best to brace her head and neck as she rolled to the shoulder of the road.

She could hear the screech of brakes as he completed the stop. Heart pounding in her ears, body aching from the fall, Erynn stood and started to run. She had to get away from him.

The woods. He would be able to see attempts at escape she made from the road and could just follow her, grab her again. This time, she suspected, he'd kill her where she stood. Not attempt any kind of abduction again.

Ever.

Erynn pushed her way into the forest, around tall spruces, her feet quiet against the forest floor. She heard nothing behind her, but that didn't mean he wasn't following. She sped up her pace, desperate to find safety, keeping her body low to the ground to avoid being seen among the trees. She must not be far from either Moose Haven or Seward, because those were the only places that had trees this tall. This part of Alaska was the northernmost rain forest in the world.

Strange, the facts that came to her mind when she was running for her life.

Tripping over a root in the trail caused her to lose her balance, but only for a minute. Erynn forced herself to focus, to pretend she was back in the academy trying to prove herself equal to or better than the few men who had given her a hard time for being a woman in their world. Most of the men had been encouraging. But that small group? They'd given her a reason to push herself harder, to accept nothing less than her best from herself, especially in areas where they expected her to be weak, like the physical agility test.

That was the determination she needed now, she told herself as she tried to take the thickest, most overgrown routes possible. But the vegetation was largely gone in the winter; only the thickness of the spruce forest saved her from being exposed altogether. The snow was largely melted in this area from a recent warm wind, or maybe there hadn't been much because of the canopy, so any footprints she was leaving would be minimal.

Still no sounds behind her, no cracking branches, not even a whisper of wind.

The silence was overwhelming, but it was what she wanted to hear right now.

It meant she had a chance. A flicker of hope.

When she'd run for a solid half hour, Erynn felt in her pockets. Her phone. Was there any chance…?

She felt its familiar rectangular shape in her jacket pocket. *Thank You, God.* Not just for the phone but for the fact that she had dressed more warmly than she'd needed to, to sweep the front porch. Otherwise she'd be concerned about the dangers of exposure. It wasn't their coldest winter; the weather forecast she'd checked this morning had put temperatures in the midtwenties all day, but it was still cold enough to suffer hypothermia if someone wasn't prepared for it.

Phone in hand, Erynn looked for a more sheltered place where she could stop, see if she could get service to call Noah. Text him. Blow up his Facebook with messages.

She needed him to come. Wanted a man to rescue her, for only the second time in her life, the first being when she'd thought Officer and Mrs. Cooper were heroes disguised as a normal couple who didn't mind adopting a daughter nearly finished with high school.

When she'd hidden herself as well as she could, Erynn slid the phone from her pocket. No service. She squeezed her eyes shut. Felt one small tear escape.

And then she stood again. Because if she had heard it once in the short time she'd had Officer Mack Cooper as her dad, she had heard it a thousand times: Coopers don't quit. And she was a Cooper through and through. Owed it to him to be a good one.

She hurried through the woods, not sure if the killer was following her or if he'd given up for now.

The woods seemed to grow thinner.

Erynn's heartbeat quickened as she wondered again how near she was to Moose Haven, what she'd see in front of her.

It was a gravel road leading to a campground. Erynn looked to her right, toward the highway. She didn't know how far off it she was. A quarter of a mile? Maybe more? It was hard to judge with all the trees she'd moved past, with how the cold had seeped through her pants and made her legs feel like ice.

She ducked back into the safety of the forest, but traveled perpendicular to the road until she was deep enough in to see a sign. Moose Creek Campground.

She'd not been unconscious as long as she'd feared. They were twenty minutes or so out of Moose Haven, not far past the bridge where she'd almost been killed earlier in the week.

"Thank You, God," she whispered out loud, conscious of the fact that without His intervention, she'd never have made it even this far.

Would anyone be in the campground? It was December. Coming upon Christmas faster than she had been able to keep up with since she'd been so caught up in the case. In staying alive.

If no one was here, she'd pull out her phone, check for a signal and call for help if there was one, then wait until someone arrived. But every moment she was out here was another opportunity for the killer to find her, and Erynn wanted to get back to somewhere she had a chance of being protected.

She needed someone else to be at the campground.

The chances weren't good, but it was possible. *Please let some hardy souls be out here, enjoying winter camping.* There was a stocked lake not far, Erynn knew, whose trailhead was here at this campground. It was a popular location for ice fishing, so it wasn't altogether hopeless to think that someone might at least be parked nearby.

As long as it wasn't the man after her.

She rounded a corner, the trailhead in sight now. Two cars. *Two!* If someone could just be in one…

One was a Ford. Erynn stopped immediately when she saw it but then realized it was an SUV and the car she'd been in was a smaller sedan. She was safe. As long as she kept her eyes open to make sure the car she was hiding from didn't approach.

Was the killer familiar with Moose Haven? Might he realize walking through the woods in this direction would lead her to this campground? Erynn hoped not.

The first car was empty. The second, the SUV, had someone sitting in the driver's seat, fumbling in the seat next to them with what looked like a fishing pole.

Erynn took a breath and knocked on the window.

Startled, the driver, a woman, rolled the window down. But only halfway. Cautious. Erynn respected that, appreciated her carefulness. "Can I help you?"

"Yes." Erynn wasted no time, her words coming in breathless puffs. "I need to get to Moose Haven. Someone is trying to kill me and I jumped out of the car."

The woman's eyes widened. "Wait, I just heard on the radio— You're the trooper. The local broadcast said the Moose Haven Police issued an APB. We're supposed to look for you. I was just going to go fishing… Oh, my goodness, you're okay! I can fish another day, get in the car." She was already clicking the unlock button. Erynn didn't bother going around to the passenger side, she just climbed in the back. Sat on the floor between the seats.

"Aren't you going to buckle up?" the woman asked doubtfully as she put the car in Reverse. "You are a trooper, right? And I don't know that it's illegal to be unbuckled in the back seat, but it's definitely frowned upon." She turned toward the gravel road that led back toward the highway. Erynn shivered, afraid of what they might find ahead of them. What if the killer was waiting to attack again, watching her try to get to safety? To be this close to Moose Haven and still not be sure she could make it there...

"Listen, the man who is after me, if he sees me in your car, he'll try to run us off the road and... I don't know exactly what he'll do but I don't want him to hurt you, either."

"So you need to stay out of view."

"Yes."

"Gotcha." The woman reached for something in the passenger seat, then tossed a scratchy, green army blanket back at Erynn. "It's for an emergency. My husband always insists that I take it along just in case. I'm pretty sure hiding a woman from a crazy killer wasn't what he had in mind, but I mean, it works, right?"

Erynn pulled at the blanket until it covered all of her to her waist. If she needed to lie down and hide completely, she would, but at the moment she wanted the luxury of being able to see where they were going. "Thank you for driving me."

"No problem." The woman turned left onto the highway, toward town.

"Any sign of a dark, almost black Ford? It's some kind of sedan, whatever their latest model is."

"Nope. I just saw a red pickup, but that's the only car on this part of the road besides us right now."

Relief flooded through Erynn. "Good." She didn't say much for the rest of the ride, just kept her heart in a constant *Please, please. Thank You. Thank You* cycle of unspoken prayers.

"I need to go to the Moose Haven Police Department," she told the woman when they were entering town.

"Not the trooper station?"

Erynn shook her head. "No. Not there." Because right now she didn't just want law enforcement around her. She wanted Noah.

"Okay, will do."

For the first time in hours, Erynn let out a deep breath.

"An SUV just pulled up in front of the station and a woman got out." Clay Hitchcock stepped into Noah's office, leaned against the doorframe. "You want me to send the lady back to talk to you?"

"If it's pertinent to Erynn, yes."

Noah looked back down at the grids on his desk. He had men out searching every inch of this part of the peninsula and more ready to go when he figured out where to assign them. They'd let this guy run roughshod over their plans for long enough and now Erynn was suffering for it. Yes, Noah should have been more aggressive in the work he'd done to keep her safe in his home. He didn't know how and, logically speaking, he knew he'd done the best he could balancing Erynn's safety and his work on the case, but he needed someone to blame and he was the easiest.

Commotion in the hallway got his attention. Noah stood. "Ideas what that is?"

"No." Clay stepped out, stepped back in. "It's Erynn." And then he was gone.

Noah hurried out with him. Clay hadn't said if she was alive or...

But there she was, walking down the hallway toward him, red hair wet and tangled around her dirt-smudged face, her clothes looking like they'd seen some rough wear.

"Erynn." His voice was barely more than a whisper.

She saw him at the same time, picked up her pace.

He opened his arms, not able to possibly care less at that moment about how people around him would perceive his actions. He just wanted to touch her, know for himself that she was okay.

Tears shone in her eyes, Noah could see as she got closer, and he wrapped his arms around her. She came willingly, tucking her head into his chest. He could feel her quiet sobs, understood the weight of them. She'd come close to losing her life. He had almost lost her, a fact he needed to face.

Something about the way he'd been investigating had to change. Because Noah couldn't let this happen again.

"Let's go in my office, get a statement from you and then take you home."

She looked up at him and nodded.

It took a couple of hours for Noah to finish filling out the paperwork this new development warranted and, while he did, Erynn slept on the couch. He'd had one of the EMTs come check her out and they'd pronounced her healthy enough. Her bruises hurt, he could tell by the look on her face when they'd examined her, but she was remarkably strong. Once the EMT left, though, he'd noticed the tired lines around her eyes and suggested she lie down. For the first time she hadn't argued about resting. He'd also been able to talk to the woman who'd brought her in and thanked her profusely.

Erynn had seen the killer, she'd told him. But all they knew was that his build was on the slight side. His head hadn't reached the top of the headrest, that was all Erynn was sure of.

The frustration that she'd been so close and still couldn't give them anything solid to get an identification on the man... he heard it in her voice. While he wished she'd seen more, too, he was mostly glad she was safe.

They'd catch the killer. Soon. He was determined.

He was just gathering his things to take Erynn back to his house when Clay walked in again.

"How are you doing?"

Noah didn't answer right away, just considered the words before shaking his head. "I could have lost her."

Clay glanced at Erynn's sleeping figure on the couch then looked back at Noah. "Does she know? How you feel, I mean?"

He nodded.

"And?"

"It's complicated." The truth was, Noah wasn't sure why. All he knew was that while he'd march straight down to a church or a courthouse today and pledge his life to Erynn, she was holding back. Hesitant about something. Noah himself? The idea of falling in love?

What he wouldn't give for a place when she'd have

the time and space to figure that out instead of having to run, hide and fight for her life.

"You'll get there," Clay said with more confidence than Noah felt. "I wanted to pass on the message that Trooper Pederson is on his way to Anchorage by helicopter. They're taking him to Providence to treat his injuries, but so far he's in stable condition."

That was good to hear. Noah nodded. "Thanks. And thanks for…everything."

"Anytime." Clay walked out and Noah turned his attention to waking Erynn.

Sleepy as she was, she woke quickly and followed him down the hallway and out to where his car was parked. He'd moved it even closer to the back door so he could get her inside and back to his house quickly.

The drive home was quiet. Neither of them seemed to have much to say. Given the weight of a day like this one, what was there to be said? Noah wished he could promise her it wouldn't happen again, but hadn't he thought it wouldn't happen the first time?

They had to wrap up this case.

Noah's phone rang just as he finished that thought. He glanced at Erynn, who was looking out the window, and reached for his phone.

"Hello?"

"Chief Dawson, Danny Howard here."

"Officer Howard, how can I help you, sir?"

"It's about how I can help you. I know we talked earlier about those notes I have… I've been thinking you really may be right that there's something in there that could help you with this investigation. I reckon you ought to make your own decision about how involved you want to be in this case. It's dangerous, but I don't want to stand in your way."

When they'd spoken earlier, the man had promised to give Noah information but had seemed hesitant. This was the best break he could have had in the case today, short of the man who'd abducted Erynn sitting in a jail cell. That would have been the best option. But he'd take this for now.

"Yes, sir, I'd love to get the information from you. Could you fax it to me? Or scan it?"

"I'm afraid I can't."

Noah waited for an explanation.

"Mack trusted me with these, made it very clear I was to protect them. I don't feel comfortable sending them when criminals are able to do all kinds of inter-cepting emails and other things."

So the man was a mild conspiracy theorist. It made getting the notes trickier, but not impossible. Noah moved to his next option. "Can I meet you in Anchor-age?"

Erynn whipped her head around to look at him.

"To tell you the truth, son, I'm actually on my way to Moose Haven now. If you want the notes faster, we could meet…say at the Trail Lakes parking lot, the big new one off the side of the road? Do you know where I mean?"

He did. "Yes, sir."

"Okay, I'll see you there in about an hour."

Noah bypassed the turn to his house and glanced at his dashboard to make sure his car was filled with gas. It was.

"Now are you going to tell me what's going on?" A glance at Erynn told him a little bit of light had returned to her eyes. She couldn't keep up this cycle, Noah knew. Eventually it was going to be too much for her, as it would be for anyone.

"We're meeting your dad's partner."

"Danny Howard agreed to talk to you?" Erynn shook her head. "That's practically discrimination."

"You mean he wouldn't talk to you?" Noah asked, thinking he grasped the meaning of her mumbled statement. And, no, while it wasn't necessarily right, he couldn't blame the man for not wanting to share what he felt was dangerous information with Erynn. Howard would feel a sense of loyalty to his former partner, and not helping the man's daughter walk straight into danger was probably part of that.

Well, hopefully it wouldn't affect his willingness to share with Noah what he knew.

"No, but it's okay."

It didn't sound particularly like it was, but Noah could tell when he didn't need to push a subject further.

"This is where I jumped, I think," Erynn said when they were about fifteen miles out of Moose Haven, not far past the campground.

Noah looked at the curve in the road, could understand how if the killer had slowed to avoid losing control, this would have been Erynn's best option. He glanced at Erynn now. "You're sure you're okay?"

She nodded. "As much as is possible right now."

Empty promises echoed in his mind.

We're going to find him. It's going to be okay. Don't worry, he can't get away with this forever.

But he didn't dare say any of the thoughts aloud because if they sounded hollow to him, he could only imagine how they would sound to Erynn. This had eaten up years of her life and who knew how much of her peace. What decisions had she made because of this? She had alluded days ago to understanding Kate's sudden career change. Noah hadn't talked to his sister much about it, hadn't quite understood her decision to join the troopers. Maybe a conversation there would help him understand Erynn.

It wouldn't hurt, anyway.

"There's the parking lot," Erynn commented. Noah had already seen it, knew right where it was, but understood her comment as a way to deal with her growing unease. His matched what she probably felt, his stomach churning and his throat closing so it was harder for him to breathe. The human body responded in amazing ways to stress, some Noah had learned to appreciate over the years and some he didn't particularly like but understood. This was more the second: fight or flight misapplied. Because right now the man they were after was faceless, a phantom who appeared, terrified them, stole people's lives and then disappeared again.

They needed to be able to make him into a real person, who got flustered, had to make decisions on the fly. Up until now, he'd had too much leeway. They'd been playing defense, but how did they switch to offense?

"I see a car," Erynn continued.

Noah drove over to it. "Do *not* get out, got it?" Her eyes were wide.

"What?" He glanced away from her back over to Howard's car.

"He's not in the car. He's not in the car, Noah!" She was already reaching for the door handle.

Noah climbed from his seat and looked into the passenger window of the car next to them.

Empty.

And the driver's seat, the steering wheel, the window glass on the driver's side…all were smudged with blood.

"We have to find him!"

Because seeing the body of her dad's former partner would be a good idea for her mental health, he thought dryly. But what was he supposed to do? He couldn't leave her there, but neither could he just abandon the parking lot when the man could be fighting for his life in the low, bushy trees somewhere.

Noah dialed his brother-in-law's number, told Clay to get the troopers out there.

"We have to find him. Noah, please." Erynn had already started toward one of the many narrow foot trails etched in the dirt for weary travelers to stretch their legs and berry pickers to try their luck with the bushes in the fall.

"Let's go. Stay with me." He tugged her to him, made sure they were walking close enough there was very little room to separate them.

The trail had drops of blood, too, crimson on the snowy ground, and some slight footprints—the snow didn't always give when someone stepped on it.

They followed the trail for nearly a mile when the blood abruptly stopped. Noah couldn't see evidence of any of the small trees being trampled, and there were no more tracks of any kind. His sister could have found them. She was practically a mind reader when it came to tracking people in the backcountry. Noah wasn't bad; he just didn't have that kind of gift to the same degree. Reading people, sure. At tracking he was average at best.

"We've got to get back. I don't like how isolated we are."

Erynn didn't argue—just kept quiet and close as they retraced their steps.

Was it like seeing her dad die all over again? Noah's parents had been gone for years now, but they'd at least passed relatively peacefully, in a small plane crash that had happened so quickly that he and his siblings had been assured they wouldn't have felt any pain.

Howard, however, and Erynn's dad…there were no such promises he could make about them.

"I'm sorry," he said to her as they reached the car. He shook his head. "I don't see the notes anywhere in his car, either."

"Was it unlocked? We could check closer." She looked so hopeful that Noah nodded. "You can try the door and see." He handed her a pair of latex gloves. "Be careful not to smear any of the…of the blood." He winced, hating himself for drawing attention to it, but knowing that in her upset state he hadn't wanted her to forget protocol and be responsible for destroying what could be the only evidence they had.

"Not under this seat." Erynn checked the front seat, then opened the back door, slid her hand under the bench seat. "There's something here." She felt around. "A gun case." She pulled it out. "Empty." Her disappointment was evident.

Noah looked around the open area, almost able to feel eyes on him, a crawling sensation running down his arms, his back. "We need to get out of here."

"But…" Startled, Erynn met his eyes and then nodded. "Okay."

Noah didn't want to think about how he must have looked for her to comply that quickly. But they climbed back into his car.

As they were pulling out, two trooper cars pulled in. Noah stopped and rolled down his window.

"You called this in, Chief?" one of them asked.

Noah nodded. "Yes. We were supposed to meet a man here about the Foster Kid Killer case. But he's not here."

"That's his car?"

"Yes."

"We'll keep looking."

"Thank you." Noah rolled the window back up, turned right. Not toward Moose Haven, but toward Anchorage.

"Where are you going?"

"Anchorage."

She shook her head once and glanced back out the window, her head tilted like she was looking in the rear-view mirror, back at the scene from which they'd come. "I'd thought we might need to go there to follow some leads, but not like this. Not when Danny Howard…"

Her voice choked and Noah thought he understood. Had the man not stolen enough from her over the years—he had to kill her father's partner, too? It left a bitter taste in his mouth. A feeling of defeat that he couldn't push away in himself much less in Erynn.

He had been feeling less and less confident they would solve this case without someone else being killed. Noah hated when he was right about things like this.

FOURTEEN

There hadn't been anything to say on the drive to Anchorage. Erynn had tried a couple of times, both about the case and about other subjects, but her heart wasn't in it and she guessed Noah could tell, because he didn't seem particularly interested in carrying on a conversation, either. Finding Danny's car had crushed the flicker of hope she'd felt building in her. Now she felt...nothing.

For all practical purposes, it was over. The person who had their last solid leads was dead, his body somewhere in the Alaskan wilderness.

They kept driving, Erynn's phone dinging every time they went in and out of service. It seemed to her there were more dead spots than service zones between Moose Haven and Anchorage.

As they drove out of Turnagain Pass and the road wound around over the river and into Portage—not so much a town as a glacier and a wildlife conservation center—she got service again. She glanced at her phone just for something to do—a habit that disgusted her but one she was happy to give in to right now. The phone, the digital nothingness, made her numbness feel less overwhelming. And right now she'd take anything that would.

Three new emails.

One was from her cell phone company. One from a friend from high school who'd heard Janie had died and wanted to know what Erynn knew.

One from Danny Howard. She checked the time stamp. He'd emailed her less than fifteen minutes before they'd pulled off.

They had barely missed him. Barely missed whoever had hurt or, more likely, killed him.

"Please pull over." Erynn scarcely got the words out before she lost the little bit of food she'd eaten all over Noah's floor mat. She winced, let round two flow from her, and kept going until her stomach was empty and her eyes burned from tears. So many people she'd not been able to save. Losing Danny was like losing her dad all over again. Except this time she wasn't a helpless kid. She was an adult, a law enforcement officer, and she should have been able to stop it.

God, why couldn't I? Why can't I be in the right place at the right time?

She ended her prayer, needing the distance. God cared about her. She'd been blessed with people in her life for years, who, even though they weren't her family, had taught her that, made it clear from the way He'd worked in her life. But at times like this, the feeling didn't match her reality and that made her uncomfortable. Faith was something she had been well taught. Wrestling with her own? Not so much. Did God mind her questions, her anger?

Erynn wasn't sure. Any other time she'd ask Noah,

a man whose quiet, real faith seemed always put into action. But right now she needed space from him, too.

A week ago she'd had him as a friend, occasionally a partner in investigating, and now he had a front-row seat to watch her life disintegrate. And she'd kissed him—good enough that she knew she'd never be able to pull off some kind of lame lie like she'd done it just because of the stress of the case. He knew her feelings now, just as she knew his through his words.

She was trapped. Because he had never been supposed to find out about feelings she never should have allowed herself to have. Some people were allowed a happily-ever-after.

She wasn't one of them.

She wiped her mouth with a napkin she found in Noah's glove compartment. Felt a hand on her back, rubbing. Looked over at Noah.

"It's okay, Erynn."

There was nothing to do but shake her head, feeling her whole body quiver with the exertion of what she'd just been through.

"I mean, it's not. It's awful. It's horrible. But you can't give up yet. Believe with me that maybe it could be okay."

His voice was thin, not the solid, confident force it usually was, and somehow that made Erynn trust him more. Made her want to try to have that belief.

"I'll try." Erynn blew out a breath and looked down at the mess. She then opened the car door, lifted the floor mat out of the car and did her best to deposit the... mess outside in the grass next to where Noah had pulled over. "Sorry about your car."

"It's the least of my worries. Just be okay, Erynn." She

thought she heard him whisper "please" as she shut the door and he started driving again, but she wasn't sure.

"I got an email from Danny Howard." She watched him as she said the words, saw his grip on the steering wheel tighten and his shoulders bunch. "When?"

"It came through just now, but it looks like he sent it not long before we…found his car." She struggled to keep her voice normal.

"What did it say?"

She clicked her phone screen, waited for it to open. "I haven't read it yet, hold on."

Service still wasn't the best and the email took long enough to load that Erynn could feel her stress level rising. When she opened it, her eyes scanned the message itself.

Erynn Cooper,

It's important to me that you know that I never doubted your abilities as a trooper. That's not why I kept this from you for so long. Rather it's because I felt I owed it to your dad to do my best to protect you. I guess this seemed like the best way to do it. I was wrong.

I'm sitting in the pullout, waiting to meet you, but am growing more apprehensive with every second. If I'm right and someone is coming here to do me harm, keep me from sharing this information, I'm attaching as much as I can in attachments. It's a risk, but it's one I'm willing to take and probably should have taken earlier. An old man's paranoia may have gotten the best of him, but trust me, I was doing the best I could to keep your dad's notes safe. I owed him that, he was the best partner I could have asked for. I'm sending pictures I've taken of the handwritten sheets I have. Thank you.

Her heart thudding in her chest, she opened the first attachment, the sight of her dad's handwriting making her heart leap and sink at the same time. "He wrote the notes out."

"Your dad?" Noah's voice was steady again, and he kept driving, didn't stop to make eye contact or anything.

"Yes." She didn't know why she'd expected them to be typed. Her dad had always preferred to do things by hand. He'd not trusted many people enough to input his notes into the system by typing them out after he'd brainstormed.

Erynn read the scanned note.

Connections: Foster Care

Approved Foster Home Shortage—Happened three months before the first murder. Coincidence?

All born in Alaska. Again, coincidence?

He had written something underneath that she couldn't quite decipher. It was scrawled hastily, like he'd been under pressure, maybe a time constraint when he wrote that part.

Would her adoptive mom be able to read the handwriting better than Erynn? After all, Anne had had years more practice. The thought of seeing her again overwhelmed her. Erynn wasn't proud of all the decisions she'd made after her dad's death… She was proud to have left home to join the troopers, but regretted the way she'd kept in touch with Anne only with cards.

Erynn hadn't known how else to handle her grief. But the older she got, the more she watched other people in their relationships, the more she suspected she'd not done the right thing. Would her mom forgive her?

She glanced at Noah, tried to decide how much she wanted to explain. Then again, what was the purpose of her walls now? They hadn't protected her from falling for him.

Would Noah still feel the same when he knew she'd basically abandoned the family she'd had left after her dad was killed? That she had reverted from calling Anne "Mom" to "Anne" again in her head? Sending cards for a decade, never showing her face again… It was a horrible way to treat someone. She didn't necessarily want Noah to know what a failure she was at relationships, but shouldn't he know?

In fact, maybe telling him was exactly what she should do. Then no matter how many feelings they might have for each other, Noah would understood why the two of them together could never happen.

"We need to go see Anne Cooper."

"Relative?" He had his poker face on now, unreadable.

"Adoptive mom."

She felt him tense. Didn't even need to look at him to confirm that it was true. "You call her Anne?"

See, this was why it was a good idea to let him look a little deeper, see the ugly parts of her, the parts that were broken. They would drive him away, at least back to them just being friends and occasional colleagues.

Erynn wished she was alone, wished she had the luxury of a few minutes to cry for what might have been. Instead she focused on a spot of lint on her blue jeans, flicked it off.

"I know I don't understand, Erynn, but I'm trying to. Did your adoptive mom hurt you somehow? You talk about your dad with so much love but you call your mom by her first name? Help me out here."

"You're going to need to take Rabbit Creek Road once you get to Anchorage. She lives in one of the houses up there." They were only just passing Girdwood and the Alyeska Highway. He wouldn't need those directions for half an hour at least, but Erynn didn't want to answer the questions. She'd had enough introspection, explanation, for one day.

Noah let her ignore the question—just kept driving in silence.

Erynn opened the next attachment Danny had sent. Again, her dad's handwriting felt like a familiar stab in her heart.

Look into:
Social Workers
Law enforcement
Dispatch
Firemen
EMTs

Why had he been so convinced that someone in emergency personnel was involved? Erynn wished she knew that, but he'd only written down notes and reminders, not a detailed explanation. He had expected to be able to work the case himself, she reminded herself. He had not planned to leave these as his legacy for her to finish.

And if Danny was right, he might not have wanted her to. She couldn't believe that, not really. Even if he'd said so, it was a father talking, not a police officer. He'd given his life for her safety, hers and the other kids, to try to save their lives. How could he expect her to leave the case alone?

"Do you mind telling me why we're going to see her, at least?" Noah's voice broke her focus, brought her back to reality.

"I can't make out some of his handwriting. I didn't have enough years to learn to decipher it." She almost smiled at the thought of how many times she'd heard Anne tease him about his chicken scratch. But Anne had always been able to read it. Erynn hadn't thought of her adoptive mom so much in so long, that it surprised her how much her mind was staying focused on her now. But it was. Erynn thought of the hot breakfasts she'd fixed every morning, remembered how she'd been such a calming influence on both Mack and Erynn. She'd been the perfect mom for her, and Erynn had walked away.

"Just tell me where to turn."

Erynn nodded. "Okay."

She could only hope she was right and that Anne could read it. And that their time in Anchorage brought them closer to the killer's identity.

Because time was running out.

"Turn right here." Erynn's voice was strained and Noah wondered again what the story was between her and her adoptive mom. But he'd asked once and she wasn't saying. He was not in the habit of forcing information out of people he cared about.

He made the turn, looked to her for the next direction.

"Drive about three quarters of a mile and then turn left."

She hadn't consulted her phone for directions, hadn't looked up the address, so he assumed Anne Cooper still lived in the house where Erynn had spent the end of her high school career. It felt like a glimpse into who she was that he had not been expecting but was thankful for.

In fact, it explained a lot of things so far. Like her tendency to avoid relationships and commitment. Was she afraid of getting hurt again? She'd loved her adoptive dad as fully as anyone could love a father of any kind; he knew that from the way she talked about him. Then he'd died. Was the way she'd abandoned Anne self-protection?

And was that why she kept pushing Noah away?

He didn't need her to answer to be pretty sure his conclusions were accurate. The question in his mind now was how he was supposed to convince her that, God willing, he wasn't leaving. Wouldn't abandon her. Wouldn't take unnecessary risks that could take him away from her.

She'd kissed him. That had been a huge step for her. Truthfully, he'd haul her to a church today and marry her, take care of her and love her forever, if he was sure she wanted that, too.

But that was the thing about love. It was a choice. One Noah couldn't force Erynn to make.

Please, God. Besides finding this killer and putting

*him behind bars for the next ninety to life, I also want
Erynn to be my wife—*

"This is the driveway." Her voice startled him out
of his prayer. If she had any idea the things he was
thinking of, praying for... He couldn't imagine how
fast she'd run.

"Okay." He turned and pulled up in front of a typical
hillside house—a long-fronted, A-framed prow in the
front with large windows that must provide sweeping
views of Turnagain Pass behind them. It looked like a
good place to grow up. He only wished Erynn had been
able to come there sooner, live there longer.

"Where did you live before this?" She might not answer, but he was curious, figured there was no harm
in asking.

"In a foster home with a few other kids. Well, that's
not true. I lived a couple of months in Holloway House
downtown."

"What's that?" He wasn't familiar with Anchorage,
spent as little time in the city as possible. The excess
of cars and buildings tended to make him want to drive
in the opposite direction, back to the small town of
Moose Haven and the surrounding wilderness of the
Kenai Peninsula.

"It's a house for older kids the state can't find foster
homes for." He looked over at her. She shook her head.
"It's not bad. Just sort of a group home. Well, because
it is one." She hesitated. "A couple of the kids who lived
there were among the first victims of the serial killer."

"So not great memories of there."

She shrugged. "Let's go talk to Anne."

"Did you text?" He knew she hadn't called, since
he'd been in the car with her the entire time.

"No. I just hoped she'd be home." Her voice was unreadable, her facial expression the same. Noah still wasn't sure he understood what it was costing her to show up here. But Erynn believed the note could be read by this woman, so he understood her drive to find out if it was true.

He climbed from the car, opening Erynn's door for her, partly out of chivalry and partly because it gave him the time to look around, make sure he didn't see any obvious threats. Unless they were being followed, there was no reason to believe anyone should know they were there. But he wasn't taking chances with Erynn's safety.

"Thank you," she said as she stepped out of the car. She looked at the house, face tilted upward, and sighed.

"You okay?"

Another shrug. He wasn't sure he'd ever seen her shrug so many times. He didn't like the way it spoke of defeat. She couldn't give up, not when they were finally making progress. He hadn't had the chance to look at her dad's notes yet, but could tell from the reactions she'd had to them that they were going to prove at least somewhat useful.

Please let this be the key to ending this.

She walked ahead of him to the front door, turned back. "You're coming, right?"

He stepped forward, reached for her hand and squeezed it. "Yes." He would go with her anywhere she asked him to.

Noah moved to let her hand go, but she tightened her grip. Worked for him. Together they walked up the front steps and Erynn knocked on the door.

Footsteps approached the door. Noah felt himself trying to consciously relax his muscles in the hope that it would be contagious and Erynn would be able to relax, too. She was beyond tense.

The door opened and a woman stood there. She was in her early sixties, Noah guessed, with bobbed hair that had probably once been brown but was now lighter in color and streaked with silver. She seemed like a woman who accepted her age, but not any limitations that came attached to it.

"Can I help...?" Her eyes moved from Noah to Erynn and widened. "Erynn?"

Erynn nodded. "Hello. I'm sorry it's been so long." There went that shrug again.

Anne Cooper had already wrapped her arms around Erynn in a huge hug. Anne was crying, her shoulders shaking as she sobbed.

Noah looked around again, growing uncomfortable with the amount of time they were spending standing outside. "Mind if we step inside, ma'am?"

She looked up, wiped the tears from her cheeks. "Of course, yes, it's not safe out here. Let's go inside."

Her statement caught Noah's attention. How did she know that?

"Oh, Erynn... I have so much to tell you." Anne tilted her head. "As much as I appreciate the cards, it hurts a mom's heart a bit when her baby changes her number and there's no way to communicate with her."

Noah raised his eyebrows. That was part of the story Erynn had not shared. He looked at her now but she was avoiding his eyes. And Anne's.

"I'm Chief Noah Dawson, with the Moose Haven Police Department."

"I'm Anne..." Her eyes trailed to Erynn again. "Anne Howard."

* * *

Erynn stared at Anne, tried to reconcile what she'd heard with what she'd known. Emotions waged a war with logic in her head. Howard? She'd married Erynn's dad's partner? Part of her was angry. How dare she dishonor his memory by... What, not living as a widow for over a decade? And not just as a widow but one whose only daughter had abandoned her, practically pretended the adoption had never even happened with the exception of some Christmas cards that eased her guilt.

No, Anne had been right to marry Danny if she'd fallen in love. Erynn's dad had loved him. He'd have probably been all for it, although that wouldn't have happened had he lived since Erynn knew they'd had a strong, loving marriage and neither of them would have considered divorce.

"I'm...happy for you." She meant the words. As much as she was capable of right now while experiencing this emotional overload of sorts.

"Thanks, sweetheart." Anne hugged Erynn again. "It was lonely around here for years after your dad died."

Was killed, Erynn corrected in her mind but didn't say out loud. "And now Danny..."

"We don't know what happened to him yet," Anne corrected before Erynn could say another word. The woman always believed the best, something Erynn loved about her, even if it was a quality she couldn't bring herself to emulate. It was much easier to expect the worst and be surprised if you were wrong.

The chances that he'd tangled with the serial killer and survived were abysmal. However, she hadn't seen Anne in too long and she wasn't going to be responsible for crushing her fragile hopes.

Erynn knew enough about what that felt like to hate it when it happened to anyone else. It was ironic: her struggle was the very thing she wanted to save the world from, part of what had motivated her to a career in law enforcement. She wanted to give people hope that things would be okay.

"That's part of what we need to talk to you about, Mrs. Howard." Noah spoke up, for which Erynn was thankful. Maybe her boss had been right to remove her from the case officially. She was leading with her heart, something she had never done before.

Anne tilted her head, studied Noah. "Are you the people he was heading to meet? He told me he was meeting an officer and a trooper but wouldn't say names. I assumed it was for my safety as he's typically pretty vague about things like that. Or was when he was working. He retired last year." She said the last part to Erynn, who nodded.

"Yes, he was meeting me." Noah glanced at Erynn. "And Erynn."

A few seconds passed until understanding washed over Anne's face. Erynn thought she might have paled a little, also. "Oh." She shook her head. "Come in, I think I'll make us all some coffee. If I'm understanding correctly, we have a lot of talking to do. This way." She moved from the entryway up a short set of stairs to a large open area. The mountains were visible out the front window, just like they'd always been, and Erynn immediately felt at home. Like she'd never left. But also like it had been years.

She had never imagined—okay, had *rarely* imagined— facing her past again. At least not like this, here in this house, feeling like family and a stranger all at once. She had certainly never imagined dragging Noah back into it with her.

But here she was. And here he was. And, ready or not, her past was coming for her.

FIFTEEN

The tension between Anne and Erynn fascinated Noah, especially because it didn't feel like the strain of people who'd had a falling out. He was even more sure now that his earlier assumption about Erynn pushing Anne away out of fear of getting hurt was right.

"So you're a state trooper now?" Anne shook her head, handed each of them a mug of coffee. Noah took a long, appreciative sip. Nice and strong. He could see where Erynn had gotten her love of the stuff. He liked coffee fine, but Erynn was the only one he knew who liked it strong enough to disintegrate a plastic spoon.

Erynn nodded. "Yes."

"Did you always plan—" Anne cut herself off. "Of course not. You never talked about anything like that. Did you decide because of your dad?"

He watched Erynn flinch. Someone might as well have slapped her from the way she jumped back, the way the pain flashed across her face.

"Yes. For Dad." Her voice wavered.

"Well, I'm a bit unhappy, because mothers prefer their children safe. But he would have been proud."

Noah watched Erynn, but she didn't give away much with her guarded facial expression, just nodded.

"So tell me why you needed to talk to me. I'm glad you're here, Erynn, and I'd love to catch up later, talk about if there's anything I did to upset you... But I know right now you're on a mission. And if you're going to find my husband, so I don't lose him, too..." She choked back tears. "Then I need to help you so you can be on your way and save him."

He hated to give her false hope. While Noah had been trying to hang on to some degree of optimism, he was fairly certain that Erynn's assumption that the man was dead was correct.

"It's this note." Erynn pulled her phone out of her pocket and Noah watched as she opened the email. He still hadn't seen it, so he moved farther down the couch, to the spot beside Erynn so he could read over her shoulder.

Anne was nodding as she read, looking like she'd been transported back over a decade. "Yes, I remember him talking to me about some of this."

"Dad talked to you?" Erynn's head shot up.

"Of course, sweetheart, I was his wife."

Noah watched the two of them, studied Erynn's face.

"But he didn't...keep work things from you?"

"He never shared anything that he shouldn't have. But we shared our whole lives. Made one life out of the two."

For the second time in their friendship, and in the last week, he saw Erynn start to cry. He felt like an intruder, as if his presence in the room was overstepping boundaries somehow. He didn't know why—he'd learned more about Erynn in the last few days, especially her past, than he'd ever hoped—but somehow it seemed like if he really wanted to show her that he respected her right to space he needed to give it to her.

"I'm sorry, but do you mind if I look around your husband's office? I'd love to see if there's anything in there that might hint at something we could use." Noah was taking a risk assuming there was an office and that he'd read Erynn right that she'd like to be left alone. But this was a good investigative move anyway. They could cover more ground working from two angles.

"Of course." Anne motioned up a set of stairs against the far wall. "The loft is his office. I've left it the same way since Mack's death."

"Thank you." He moved that direction, up the stairs, and noted that while he could still hear their voices, he couldn't make out what was being said.

There, he'd given Erynn what she'd wanted. Space.

He looked around the room, decided to start with the desk. The first drawer was pens, office supplies and the like. They held nothing that pertained to the case, save an empty file folder that read "Mack's Notes."

The computer on the desk caught Noah's eye. Could Danny Howard have been more of a digital kind of man? He moved the mouse and the computer woke instantly: no password. Of course not. Not if Danny and Anne lived with the kind of closeness she and Mack had enjoyed.

He clicked the email icon, brought up the man's account to take a closer look at the messages Erynn was discussing downstairs. He squinted as hard as he could, tilted his head both ways, but still couldn't get the handwriting to make sense to him, either, at least at the bottom of the first page. It was good Erynn had come here.

Hopefully in more ways than one. Because he didn't just need this case solved. He needed Erynn safe and strong, in every way. And Noah could feel that being here, looking straight down the nose of her past, was how she needed to heal.

Erynn watched Noah walk away, up into the loft, and couldn't decide if she was upset with him for leaving her without a barrier between her and Anne, or if she was grateful for the privacy.

She looked up at the woman she'd called "Mom" for years, saw tears shining in her rich brown eyes.

"How did you do it, Mom?" She stumbled over the last word, but it had slipped out before she could stop it. "How did you get through everything if you and Dad really were that close?"

"Oh, sweetie, I didn't do it on my own."

Had Erynn forgotten the way faith was integrated so deeply into every aspect of her mom's life? Maybe so. She certainly hadn't let her own sink roots as deep in the last few years. She was thankful to God for many things, tried to keep a cordial relationship with Him in church, but what she'd believed as a child about Him delighting in her, well…that seemed the stuff of fairy tales. Too much of Erynn's life had proved to her that if God wasn't cruel— and Erynn knew He wasn't—then He simply must not pay much attention to her. Or must not care overly much.

She hadn't bothered to figure out which. It had hurt too deeply either way.

"Oh."

"Don't get that look on your face. I taught you better, you know better. God gives grace, Erynn. And I handled your dad's death because I had to. Just like I'll handle Danny's if I have to, though I'm praying hard I won't."

Erynn hated that she'd likely be the one having to

break the bad news to her mother when all her prayers amounted to nothing. Just like Erynn's had when she'd begged God for a family and He'd given her one for two years, then allowed half of it to be snatched away.

"I don't want to talk about God anymore, if that's okay. I just want to know what this line says so we can go figure out who's trying to kill me."

"Of course." Anne's voice had grown distant. Anne studied the email attachment. "'Connections—foster care…'"

"I've read that part." Erynn did not need to hear it all again; she'd memorized the legible contents.

"Which part can't you read?"

Erynn leaned closer, caught a scent of warm vanilla, the lotion she remembered her mom using. Her eyes stung with tears she didn't want to shed. She'd had enough crying this week to last a lifetime. She steeled herself against it. "Right here."

"Holloway House," she read.

"That's the name of the place I stayed, not long before I came here." Erynn frowned, looked up at Anne.

"Who else was there?"

Anne's voice was quiet as usual, unwavering and confident, Erynn thought.

"A girl named Rachel. Then there was Luke. Madison. Janie. Matt. William, Sydney. Me." Chills went down Erynn's spine and she shivered with the sudden cold that had overtaken her, even though the room had been plenty warm before.

"Rachel and Luke? What happened to them?"

Erynn shook her head. "They're fine. Nothing happened to them, I just saw Luke posting on social media this morning." She frowned.

"Did anyone leave before the others? Anything like that?"

"No. Well, yes, Luke left fairly early on. But Rachel was there the whole time I was."

Her dad had to have had a reason for writing the group home down, had to have a good reason to think it could link them all together. The fact that Erynn wasn't quite able to figure out what it was implied it was the key to everything, to figuring out who had connections to all of them.

"When your dad got stuck like this, he'd go out on the back deck."

Erynn nodded. She remembered seeing him out there, and silly as it seemed to believe that being where he'd been could somehow help her, she found herself walking in that direction.

She paused at the double French doors, knowing better than to step outside. The area was sheltered by trees, but not even those were safe for her right now. At least, they couldn't assume so without checking first. Still, standing there even made her feel closer to her dad, remembering the times she'd find him out there, standing in the midnight sun in the winter, thinking, or under a fire-orange sunset sky in the summer.

Something caught in her brain, pinged an alarm.

Fire?

"The fire." Hope rose in her throat as anticipation shivered down her spine and along arms in the form of gooseflesh.

"What fire?"

She had her connection now; she was sure of it.

"Noah," Erynn called, knowing he'd leave what he was doing and come. She didn't deserve the kind of loyalty he'd always showed her, not when she held him at arm's length the way she did.

No, he deserved a woman with a past that was all roses, who could love him forever without unresolved trauma popping its head up and ruining it.

And Erynn was anything but that.

"Do you know what this note means?" Anne's eyes were hopeful but Erynn hesitated. She knew her dad had shared information with her mom, but it didn't feel right for her to do so. Not right now, especially when she didn't know what the clues meant.

"I know he believed there was a link because of Holloway House. That's all I can say for now." The apologetic shrug she offered was probably far from meaningful, but at least she'd tried.

Noah had come down from the loft and was standing nearby. She needed to tell him the entire story in the car, help him understand the links, but for now she had to get out of this house with a semi-graceful exit. With all the past between them, all the drama of Erynn having disappeared for years and showing up now...well, there wasn't much chance of that.

"You'll call?"

After the silence of the last few years, Erynn owed her at least that. She nodded. "I'll call."

"Thank you. I don't want to lose you again. It was hard enough losing your dad..." Anne's voice trailed off and as she spoke of Erynn's father, Erynn couldn't stop the question that had been dancing around in the back of her mind, even as she'd been working the case just now.

"Were you sorry?"

"Sorry?"

"That you loved Dad so much and then lost him.

Would you…? That stuff you said about two lives being one. Would you do it again, even if you knew it was going to break your heart?" Erynn's heart pounded so hard she could feel it in her forehead, which had already been starting to ache from the tension.

"Over and over. I would choose that man a thousand times. Because love opens you to hurt, yes. But love also opens you to…well, love. And it's worth it, sweetie."

Erynn nodded. Pulled her boots on and waited for Noah, who'd been right behind them walking to the entryway, but seemed to have stepped back again to give them space.

"Sorry," he said with a glance up at her, but his face was unapologetic. He was trying to bring them together or something, to get them to talk again.

Well, Erynn had tried. She couldn't do more than she'd just done. She just couldn't. The sooner they could get out of there, the better. Of course, that left her alone with Noah. Someone else she needed some distance from.

"I'm going to make sure nothing looks out of place outside." Noah stuck out a hand to Anne. "Thank you, ma'am. That helps a lot on the case and also on a personal level." His eyes met Erynn's and she felt almost like she'd burned him, the way he jerked his gaze back immediately. "I'm glad to meet Erynn's mom."

"Thanks for coming." Anne took his offered hand but pulled him into a hug. Of course she did.

Noah hugged her back, stepped out the front door.

And Erynn was once again alone with her past.

"Well…thank you for your help." Her words were jumbled, her mind confused as to the protocol to follow on a visit like this. Straddling the line between an investigation and the personal, it was tricky. She reached for the doorknob.

"Erynn?"

Erynn looked back.

"Choosing to love regardless of its capacity to hurt is something I'll never regret. With anyone I love. No matter how far away they run. Okay, sweetheart? I'll never, ever, regret you being my daughter or the love I give you every day."

In a moment that was so weighty with emotion and the promise of reconciliation, Erynn didn't know how to handle it. She shoved a hand at her face, practically swatting at her lashes to stop any tears before they formed. Nodded. She didn't want to be insulting.

She appreciated the sentiment.

Just couldn't accept it. Because Anne was stronger than Erynn. And Erynn couldn't love like that, not if it meant getting hurt again.

She said nothing, hurried out the door to the waiting car and didn't look back. Prepared to get away from this house permanently for the second time in her life.

They had only been driving for a few minutes when Noah spoke. "About your mom…"

"I don't want to talk about her."

"But don't you see? It's why you push me away, too—the fact that your dad died. Because you do the same to her." His tone was sincere, even if he fumbled over his words.

But Erynn felt like he might as well have taken a cannon to the walls of her emotional fortress and she resented it. She felt her shoulders stiffen, any positivity toward him vanish.

"Don't, Noah."

"Listen, it's something we can work through."

Work through. Like she was a puzzle. Just like she had been as a teenager when people overgeneralized about "those kids" and tried to figure out how to ensure she and her friends didn't end up like some other kids in foster care. There had been people who cared. She couldn't deny that her parents had been in that category. But there were some people who viewed them as projects—or worse, in Erynn's mind, as a "ministry." Did they not understand how insulting that could feel, to be that to someone? And here she was, a full-grown adult, and someone wanted to make her a project again.

Only this time it was someone whose opinion she cared about. Somehow that made it hurt all the more.

"You don't understand, you won't understand, and I don't appreciate you sitting around analyzing me like I'm a latent print under a magnifying glass."

"I'm not, I'm just—"

"You're just trying to figure out something you could never imagine, Noah. With your perfect family, and parents who loved you, siblings who still talk—did you know I have siblings? Biological siblings? Yeah, who knows where they are. I doubt they care where I am, either. I'll probably never know. You could not understand what my life was like, or how my mind works now." Erynn started to shake, took a deep breath and made herself finish, the words grinding out between her teeth. "And I'd appreciate it if you would stop trying."

He said nothing, just drove.

Finally. She'd finally managed after all these years to push him far enough away that she was safe from her feelings for him, knowing she'd likely just destroyed any he'd had for her.

SIXTEEN

Miles stretched on in uncomfortable silence and it was making Noah feel almost physical prickles of discomfort against his skin, like a shirt that rubbed wrong. His friendship with Erynn had never been like this, and it felt anything but natural now. So he'd pushed too hard, he could see that, but had it been necessary for her to shove back with quite that much certainty? He didn't think so.

Still, they needed to work together. Because he could do that, right? Forget that she was the woman he loved, and just be professional? Sure, he'd done it for the last few years. But that was before this case. Before it had felt for a minute like the last of Erynn's emotional walls had tumbled down. Before they'd kissed.

He could still feel the pressure of her lips against his, if he let himself think about it.

But for now he wouldn't. Couldn't. He was driving toward Anchorage like they'd planned, and he knew Erynn knew where she wanted to go, but he didn't.

"So what did the words say? Could she tell?"

"Holloway House."

The group home where she'd lived before coming to be with the Coopers. "You mentioned that place to me earlier, right?" He wanted to make sure he'd remembered correctly.

Erynn nodded. "We all—those of us the Foster Kid Killer has killed, and me—lived there at the same time, along with two other kids."

"Did anything happen to them?"

"No. But one of them moved out before the rest of us did, and another one, Rachel, would leave relatively often for sleepovers with a friend from school. She wasn't there the night the house caught fire."

"So it's that specific? Not just those of you who were foster kids in the house, but those who were living there at the time of a fire?" No wonder they'd had a difficult time figuring out the connection between the foster kids. How Erynn had come to that conclusion, he didn't understand but was willing to accept that it might just be one of those things that had come to her and made sense at the time.

Because God had brought her to the answer? Maybe. There had been too many instances in this case where he'd seen God working for him to discount the possibility.

"So now we're looking at everyone who was there that night," Erynn added.

"Staff?"

"I don't know why staff would only target the group that was there for the fire, but, yes, we shouldn't rule them out. But mainly emergency personnel who were there that night."

Noah thought the idea had merit, but how were they going to figure out who was present on the night of an incident that had taken place over a decade before? If police had realized the connection at the time, maybe records of who was there that night could have been preserved. Had they known?

"Were there any more pages of your dad's notes?" he asked Erynn. "You still haven't told me what those said."

"Oh, I'm sorry. I forgot. Just ideas for how we were connected, a list of the people he wanted to check out."

"Names?"

He saw Erynn shake her head out of the corner of his eye. "No names, just professions. EMTs, Dispatch, law enforcement, firemen, social workers."

"So we don't know if he made the connection to the night of the fire at Holloway House, but he was on the right track."

"Since this is why he was killed, I think he was more than on the right track—he just didn't leave us any solid proof of that, or write anything definitive down."

"So do we go by the Anchorage Police Department first, see if they've got records of that call and who responded? Their dispatch would have handled it, but I doubt records go back that far."

"Yes, I want to go there." She looked away from him, looked back out the window, and he felt the distance building between them again. She'd dropped her guard, just for a minute, when they were discussing the case, but she'd caught her mistake and corrected it.

The drive to the Anchorage Police Department wasn't bad and they were there in less than half an hour. Noah pulled into the parking lot and looked over at Erynn.

She nodded in his direction. "I know, you get to take the lead."

That wasn't what he'd been thinking at all. He'd actually been just trying to absorb the sudden break in the case, had been wondering if they were finally closing in on whoever had been behind all of this.

Wondering if Erynn would change her mind about the two of them when things settled down.

All things he needed to mentally work through another time, because right now he needed to focus.

"I'll take the lead since you're not officially on the case but, Erynn, don't forget we've gotten this far because of you. You're extraordinarily good at what you do."

She nodded once, stepped out of the car and left him scrambling to follow. They made it inside the police department without incident, and Noah spoke to the woman working the front desk.

"Is Officer Reed in?" He should have had Erynn text his brother-in-law from the car, but he hadn't remembered he had a personal connection to the department until about the time he'd pulled into the parking lot.

"He is. Could I get your name? Then I'll get him up here for you."

Micah Reed walked into the lobby not five minutes later, grinning. "Noah, hey! I should have known you'd be up here eventually. The Ice Maiden case, right?" He looked from Noah to Erynn. "How's that going?"

Noah didn't even know how to answer that. So he just cut to the chase. "We've realized it has some connections to another case APD worked years ago, the Foster Kid Killer. Long story short, we've found what connected the victims in that case and we're close to a suspect, but we need some help."

"Let's head over to Records." Micah's face had lost the grin and taken on a focused look. Noah could see why the guy was such a good match for his sister Kate. She had this same ferociously focused work mode, although for years she'd used it in Search and Rescue.

"Here we are. This is Lisa, she's one of our records technicians, and she can help us find what you're looking for, assuming the files were digitized by the year you're looking for."

Twenty minutes later, they had a list of names written on a yellow legal pad. The sheet torn off, they were ready to make a plan.

Responding Officers: Danny Howard, Mack Cooper, Rich Evans
Firefighters: Station 6 Night Crew
Paramedics: Annaliese Watkins, Devin Wyatt

"Where do you want to start?" Noah asked Erynn when they were back in his car. His heart was pounding, his palms were sweaty and he had that end-of-the-tunnel feeling that this part of a case always gave him. They were close, and he knew it, could feel it, but he had no guarantees they'd make it out of whatever happened next alive. He wanted those guarantees, would have given a great deal for them, but as it was, life didn't work that way. All he could do was hope. And pray.

And listen to Erynn, whose input had proved so valuable over the years.

"It's going to take some work to figure out exactly who was on the Station 6 Night Crew all those years ago, so let's save the firefighters for last."

"We know two of the responding officers. So we need to check out Rich Evans and the EMTs?"

"Yes."

"Who first?"

Noah watched as Erynn glanced down at her watch then looked up at him again. "Rich Evans doesn't come back on shift for another few hours," she told him. "I asked Micah while we were inside."

"So, the paramedics?"

Erynn nodded.

"I'll make the call."

The Station 6 Fire Department had also provided the EMTs. Noah made the call and explained that he needed to talk to a few people.

The woman who'd answered and introduced herself as the station's battalion chief asked, "Could you do the interviews at the station? Some of the men you've mentioned are retired now, but they could come here easily. Most of them live close, and some of the guys still work here and they're on shift right now."

Noah covered the mouthpiece with his hand and looked to Erynn. "You don't mind going to the fire station, do you?"

She shook her head.

"That would be fine. We will be there soon, thanks."

Noah ended the call, waited for Erynn to say something. "You nervous?" he finally asked her. He wasn't sure he'd seen her nervous many times in their friendship, but she was behaving strangely now.

"I was thinking about Danny Howard."

He could see that. "Is it weird that he married your mom?" Too late, he caught how he'd referenced Anne. Was that the right term to refer to her? He didn't know and hated to risk offending Erynn.

If she was offended, it didn't show. Maybe that was

how she thought of Anne, when she wasn't trying too hard to protect herself from feelings.

"No, actually. Once I thought about it, it's nice. I just hate that he's dead, too, you know?"

"I don't think he is." Noah hadn't realized he'd thought it till the words were out of his mouth and realized now it was true.

"Why?"

"Because we didn't find a body. This serial killer never goes to that much trouble hiding a corpse. The fact that Danny Howard wasn't where we thought he'd be is a good sign."

She seemed to consider it. "You could be right. Is someone looking for him, do you think?"

Noah had made sure of it hours ago. She didn't need to know details, though, so he just nodded.

Once they were at Station 6, on the east side of town, he pulled into the parking lot in front of the station and they went to the door.

"Welcome." A tall woman who looked to be in her early fifties answered the door. "I'm Chief Elaine Murphy, we spoke on the phone."

"Moose Haven Police. Chief Noah Dawson." He stuck out his hand, shook hers. "Thank you, Chief Murphy, for letting us come by today."

She nodded once. "I don't like the idea that anyone we have here could be responsible for any of the crimes you're investigating, and I don't think anyone is, but this is the quickest and best way to prove that." She studied Noah for a minute, then looked to Erynn and nodded again. "I've got a fire truck out at the moment, so I thought you could just use that empty bay to conduct your interviews."

Noah nodded, not wanting to cause any more trouble than just their presence already had. "That will work fine."

"Any particular order you want me to send them out to you in?" Chief Murphy asked.

"Anything is fine."

They interviewed two firemen, neither of whom raised Noah's suspicions at all. Both men remembered the fire and remembered the kids, but did not seem emotionally invested. Noah was expecting that their killer would have been passionate about that night one way or another, as it had apparently triggered something in him that resulted in his becoming a killer.

"Next one," he said when Chief Murphy walked in, shaking her head as she left again.

A woman entered the bay area. A paramedic, judging by her uniform. "I'm Annaliese Watkins. I heard you wanted to speak to me about the fire at Holloway House? That was years ago. Fifteen or so?" She shook her head. "I'd just started this job." She smiled a little. "Literally, that was my first week."

Well, this was finally getting interesting. Someone who'd been under a lot of pressure, in a new job, seen something that could have been dramatic...?

It still didn't play out the way Noah would have expected, and that rubbed him wrong, but he was desperate for a lead. Any lead.

"Do you remember—?"

His words were cut off by the *pop, pop, pop* of close-range rifle fire. "Get down!" he yelled to Erynn and Annaliese. The chairs they were in, portable folding ones, clattered to the ground as they hit their knees. Noah looked around the bay. Empty. He didn't see anything.

Glass shattered somewhere, but he couldn't figure out where because the lights in the station flickered off. Came back on. Something to be thankful for.

He scanned the area again. Glass had been broken at the top of one of the bays. Shot out?

An alarm sounded. Noah tried to stay in front of Erynn, to keep her from getting shot. There had been a break: five seconds, then ten without shots fired. Did that mean it was over?

"Noah…"

Erynn's voice was weaker than it should have been. Fear grabbed him, shook him with unrelenting force. If something had happened to her…

He turned around.

She was bleeding, the blood staining the blue of the jeans on her upper thigh crimson. He looked at her eyes, basic EMT classes he'd taken before coming to the forefront. Her color was good, breathing seemed normal. Shock wasn't a threat right now, but if they didn't get that seen to…

"Is everybody okay? We heard the shots." The chief ran into the room, a paramedic they hadn't met yet on her heels. "Chief Dawson?"

"No. Erynn's bleeding." He glanced over at Annaliese, who'd huddled behind a plastic chair and was now crying. "And your paramedic here needs attention, too." Noah needed Erynn's injury seen to, and the hysterical woman beside them wasn't going to do anyone any good.

"I'll take care of her." The Chief nodded, started speaking to the other woman in calm tones. After a minute, he helped her out, leaving Noah, Erynn and the male paramedic alone in the bay.

"Gunshot in the upper thigh?" The male paramedic motioned to the truck parked one row over. "Can she move this way? No, of course not. I can bring things to her, it's fine."

Noah knelt next to Erynn. "Are you okay?" He met her eyes, waited until she willingly met his and nodded.

"I'm going to be fine."

He wished he were sure. Her leg was losing more blood than he was comfortable with, but he was still hopeful it might just be a bad graze. They could still finish the interviews… Was that what was best for Erynn, though?

"We can go back to Moose Haven…" Noah offered but trailed off. She wanted this case over as much as he did, but he felt like he had to offer. Thankfully she smiled, shook her head.

"No, I need to see this through to the end."

If only her words didn't sound so foreboding to him. *The end* held too much finality right now for a man who had just watched the woman he loved get shot.

Erynn's leg stung, her pride along with it, but she tried to focus on her breathing as she waited for the male paramedic to finish gathering whatever supplies he needed to come back to her.

While she waited, she glanced at her watch again. Just another hour or so and they could go back to the police department and interview Rich Evans, the man she still wanted to talk to, there. One of the people they were talking to today had talked to her dad, been the last one to see him alive.

The one to end his life.

Erynn felt her face heat, the anger threatening to

overpower her. It wasn't fair. She'd never, ever, made peace with the injustice of it all, never would.

"Okay, let's see what's going on here."

Just that fast she lost track of the other sounds around them, which became a dull blur in the background. That voice, she knew it. She'd heard it before.

She hadn't reacted this way to Annaliese's voice and the paramedic had been at the fire. Why was that?

Erynn didn't know. But it didn't stop the chills from running down her arms, either.

Noah must have noticed her discomfort. Or something else had caught his attention, because he was studying the man, too. "Are you Devin Wyatt, by chance?"

"Yes." He was cutting a piece of gauze.

Erynn watched the scissors in his hand. Swallowed hard. She needed medical attention, she realized that, and she didn't have a solid reason for refusing it from this man. Other than that technically everyone at this station who had responded to the fire that night was a suspect and he...

He was the one she was favoring right now.

As Erynn waited, he picked up a syringe. "We're going to numb the area..." He reached for her.

"No." She shook her head, shoved her hands down onto the cool floor of the bay to scoot away from him, but he kept moving toward her, his mouth set in a line.

"Noah!" She yelled because she didn't know what else to do, and Noah reacted instantly, his hand coming up to stop the syringe. Devin Wyatt fought him, the two men ending up in a tangle on the floor.

In that moment Erynn wanted to rewind time, to go back to days before today when she'd been truthful with Noah, at least with her actions. When she'd been kissing him rather than pushing him away. When she'd been honest about the way he completely had her heart.

Because now she might be too late. And she didn't want to be.

God, help.

Erynn had her gun in a concealed holster but it wouldn't do her any good now; she couldn't get a shot without risking hitting Noah. Besides, it wasn't the way she wanted to see this man brought to justice. Instead she tried to stand, look around for another weapon in the room. She settled on a helmet sitting on a chair not far away. She threw it at Wyatt, but it was a feeble attempt, she knew that.

Erynn looked back at the men, moved into the fight and hit Wyatt in the face. He threw a hand up and managed to smack her in the leg, tripling the pain she was already in. She stumbled backward, hand against her thigh. She pulled it away and looked at it. Red. Deep red. The movement had aggravated the wound even more. She took a gasping breath, fought against the haze threatening to overtake her. Another glance at Noah showed her he was losing, or at least not winning.

Erynn knew she couldn't lose him. But she also knew she didn't have the strength to do much to help.

She looked up at the truck in front of her. Did they leave those unlocked? If she climbed up, could she hit a button to activate the sirens, get someone to help them? She felt in her back pocket. Or 9-1-1? Would that get people there faster?

She opened the phone, dialed. "Station 6. I'm having an emergency," she said as soon as someone picked up, then threw the phone down and hurried to the truck. It didn't take much work to find the siren and she pressed it.

Gasping against the pain in her leg, she hurried back to where the men were fighting, the noise overwhelming the garage and people flooding in. "Help," she managed to say, pointing to Noah. "It's Wyatt. He's the guy we're after."

And then she couldn't keep her eyes open anymore.

SEVENTEEN

The hospital was one of the last places Noah would have chosen to spend Christmas Eve, but since he was there with Erynn, waiting for her to be discharged, he wasn't going to complain.

Devin Wyatt had confessed to everything more than once. First, when the other firemen had swarmed the garage, thanks to Erynn's quick thinking, and helped Noah subdue him, and second, when the Anchorage police had arrived.

He'd done it for their own good, he'd said. He'd been a foster kid, too—something Erynn's dad had discovered when looking into the backgrounds of those connected to the kids from Holloway House. He'd felt alone, felt like life was always going to be against him. When he'd responded to a fire at that kids' home, it had brought back his own childhood trauma and he'd felt like he was saving them from theirs. At first. After that it had become a challenge. A purpose for his life—to kill all the ones he'd been part of helping that night. To stop them from suffering further, going through life in as much pain as he'd experienced.

It was sick. And Noah had almost been glad Erynn

had been unconscious for it. She could read the official report, of course, but it was still different than hearing a man scream his confession as he was hauled away.

Either way, it was over.

Mostly. He was still waiting to hear from the team sent out to search for Danny Howard. He wasn't giving up until they found a body. *Please, God.* The words came easily. Believing God cared about details like that, and was actively involved, was easier now that he'd seen God bring Erynn through what he had.

Unlike Wyatt, whose traumas had broken him, whose hurts had festered into something evil, Erynn's had made her determined. A better woman.

One he didn't deserve but was going to ask again, just one more time, for a chance at winning her heart.

"How are you feeling?" he questioned for about the fifth time since she'd been admitted yesterday. Though it had only been a graze, they'd wanted to observe her overnight due to everything she'd been through, and were being extra cautious.

Erynn glared at him, looking completely unthreatening from where she lay on the hospital bed, underneath several blankets. "Like I'm tired of being here. It's not enough I get taken off the case, I pass out before we finish it, have to hear the story from you and then end up in the hospital?"

"But you're alive."

"It was a graze, Chief Dawson." She rolled her eyes. "My living was never a question. In fact, they mostly brought me here as a precaution. They're discharging me soon and sending me home."

Maybe her living hadn't been in question because of the gunshot. But for the last few weeks in general?

Yes, it had been a very real question. Noah was looking forward to shrugging off the weight of it, but didn't quite know how yet.

"You're okay."

Erynn nodded, looked away from him.

Noah's heart sank, feeling her rejection before he'd officially offered anything…well, again at least. He guessed he didn't have to know why. If she didn't want him…

"Noah?"

He met her eyes. They were brimming with tears.

"What's wrong? Do you need me to call the nurse? Are you in pain? Do you—?"

"You've been my best friend since I moved to Moose Haven. I haven't had a best friend since fifth grade when I was put in foster care and moved around so often. I joined the troopers to find out who killed my dad. I'm…"

"What are you doing?"

"I haven't been honest with you. It's time."

Noah shook his head. "You're not dying, I thought we established that."

"But you wanted to get to know me…"

"And I do. I will." He moved to her, picked up one of her hands and held it in his for a minute before smiling then bending to kiss it.

As he did, he looked up at her. She grinned slowly and so did he.

"So you don't have to know it all right now?"

"No, I'm perfectly happy to get to know you over time. Better and better."

She frowned. "Sounds awfully patient for a man who once told me he loved me in the middle of a murder investigation, on a hike while we were walking to go find a body."

"Maybe I've learned something about patience since then."

"Maybe I didn't want you to." She widened her eyes pointedly, raised an eyebrow. Waited.

Surely she wasn't giving him permission to finish that conversation, to talk about their very real feelings. But the longer he looked at her face, the more he thought maybe she was.

"Erynn…"

"Noah…"

They spoke at the same time and she laughed. He loved that sound, could listen to it every day for the rest of his life. "You first," he offered, stepping back from her bedside.

"Noah," she started again, "there is one thing about me that I haven't wanted you to know that I do want to tell you now. If it's okay." She looked shy. He didn't remember her ever looking so hesitant before. Man, he could study her expressions, the lines of her face, her eyes, for a hundred years and never get tired.

"Oh, yeah?" he asked slowly. "What's that?"

"I love you." Her voice was steady, sure and beautiful, and words had never sounded so good.

"Erynn?"

"Yeah?"

"I love you, too. Always have. Always will."

"Noah?"

"Yeah?"

"Then why aren't you kissing me?"

He stepped up to the bed, bent and brushed a kiss across her lips.

"You call that a kiss?" she asked when he was done. But she was every bit as breathless as he was, and he'd bet her heart was also beating too fast.

"I'll call it a down payment on a kiss. How about I give you a real one when you're standing?"

"You really love me?"

"I do."

She smiled at him, a flicker of mischief in her eyes. "I like the sound of that."

"Of me loving you?" he teased, pretending not to catch any hint.

"That, too."

He couldn't help it; he bent and kissed her again. "Erynn?"

"Yes?"

"What do you think about marrying me?" The question slipped from his lips before he could analyze it. Maybe it was bad timing, but then again, he'd not had good timing their entire relationship. Why start now? He held his breath, waited for her answer.

"I think it sounds like a very good idea."

"So that's a yes?"

"Oh, it's more than a yes. It's a definitely."

And he bent to kiss her again.

The next day—Christmas Day—fire burned bright in the fireplace at Moose Haven Lodge when Mr. and Mrs. Noah Dawson returned from the short ceremony at the Moose Haven Bible Church to be met by his family. Noah's siblings would have liked to have been at the actual wedding, Erynn knew, but he'd understood her desire for something with no fuss, only the pastor present, and no hurt over not having relatives there for her.

Or maybe he'd just wanted to get married sooner than the typical time frame of most engagements and, when in the car on the way home from Anchorage yesterday, she'd suggested eloping, he'd taken her up on it.

Erynn didn't know. All she knew now was that she was married, there was a simple gold band on the fourth finger of her left hand and she had a promise from her husband to buy something sparkly as an engagement ring when they went to Anchorage next. Personally, she could not care less if she never saw the city again, with all the hurt it had caused her, but she knew facing her fears, the ghosts from her past, was the best way to move past them.

"Erynn, you're back!" Summer was all smiles, her gift of hospitality fully exercised at the inn on this Christmas morning.

"Wouldn't have missed the Dawson family Christmas." Their large family gathering at the holidays was practically a subject of Moose Haven lore, and while they'd invited Erynn before, she'd never felt like she fit. Now they were her family.

She'd thank God for them every day, as long as she lived.

Speaking of family... Erynn's grin spread wider. Her last-minute text to Anne last night had gone unanswered, and she'd assumed she and Danny already had plans for Christmas, or wanted to stick close to his doctors. But there they were, in two of the lodge's large brown chairs. "You came!" She hurried over to them, letting go of Noah's hand.

"Of course we did, sweetheart." Anne stood. "You're our daughter. You've always been mine, always will be." Her arms were around Erynn then, and she didn't fight the embrace. If this woman wanted to choose her again and again, Erynn was done fighting it. She could trust her mother's love, just like Noah's, like God's.

She'd never get tired of that realization.

"Thanks…Mom." The word she'd hardly spoken in a decade tumbled from her lips and Erynn felt a tear slide down her cheek. It was a happy tear. A cleansing tear.

She turned to the man who had almost given up his life for hers. She still couldn't believe Danny Howard had been found alive near where his car had been, but here he was in the flesh, though looking older than when she'd seen him last.

He opened his arms and she stepped into them, also accepting his hug. She hadn't expected more tears, but there they were, as the man who'd been a brother in blue to her father made it clear with his actions that while Mack could never be replaced, Danny would be there for her, like her dad would have been.

She stepped back, releasing her hold on him and smiling. "Thank you."

Erynn felt a hand on her arm and turned, found herself looking into Noah's eyes. Her *husband*. That one was going to take some getting used to, but she was going to enjoy every minute of it.

"I missed you," he said.

She laughed. "It's been five minutes."

"Emma made this for us." He held out his hand, showed her a Christmas ornament made out of a tiny slice of wood. On the circle was *Noah + Erynn* in a gorgeous, cursive script.

"Emma *made* this?"

"Yes." Noah's mouth twisted up at the corners. "*Last*

Christmas, apparently. She and everyone else have just been waiting for us to realize it."

Oh, she'd realized it, all right. She'd have had to have been devoid of every single one of the five senses to not have felt the chemistry between her and Noah. Erynn had known it was there almost from the moment she'd stepped into town and had him walk into her office for the first time. She'd just run from it.

It turned out, you couldn't run from love.

Noah had proved that to her. His family had, too. Anne had. Even Danny.

And God, most of all, had reminded her that His love was powerful, inescapable.

Erynn was thankful.

"Should we go put this on the tree?" She smiled up at Noah and let him guide her to the tall Kenai Peninsula spruce tree that one of the family had cut down for the celebration. It reached to the top of the living room's vaulted ceiling, the perfect level of grandness to celebrate a holiday that, this year, meant more to Erynn than any other she could remember.

"You can do the honors," Noah said to her as they approached.

Erynn found a relatively bare spot and hung it up.

"Hey, you bumped my four-wheeler." Nine-year-old Luke, Noah's nephew—*their* nephew, Erynn had to remind herself—laughed and rehung his ornament, then ran back to his parents. Emma and Tyler smiled at her. Erynn watched them take each other's hands and meet each other's eyes. That was probably going to end with a kiss, mistletoe or not.

Erynn stared up at the tree, at the twinkling lights, reminding her of hope, then looked around at the room.

Summer and Clay were laughing at something one or the other had said. Across the room the door creaked open. "We made it!" Erynn heard Kate call.

Erynn was at peace, having decided to step out of her role with the troopers. It had been her passion, but she'd gone past that, made it an obsession, finding who had killed her dad. Now that she'd done so, she needed a break. Maybe she'd go back to law enforcement in the future, but for now she needed a break. Time to figure out who she was, without this case hanging over her head.

Noah had supported her decision, though he'd also told her she was an incredible law enforcement officer and he would support her if she went back one day.

Her eyes drifted back to Luke, who stood by his parents, and noticed the little bump under Emma's sweater. They were expecting their second. It made Erynn wonder if maybe next Christmas it would be her who was pregnant.

"It seems you aren't without a family, after all." Noah pulled her to his side, kissed the top of her head, and she looked up and smiled.

"It seems, Noah Dawson, that you're right."

"I think that's the first time you've ever said those words to me." A grin teased the edges of his mouth and he laughed. Erynn made a face then laughed, too.

"I think you should stop talking and kiss me," she said to him.

And he did.

* * * * *

Get 4 FREE REWARDS!

We'll send you 2 FREE Books plus 2 FREE Mystery Gifts.

Love Inspired® Suspense books feature Christian characters facing challenges to their faith... and lives.

FREE Value Over **$20**

YES! Please send me 2 FREE Love Inspired® Suspense novels and my 2 FREE mystery gifts (gifts are worth about $10 retail). After receiving them, if I don't wish to receive any more books, I can return the shipping statement marked "cancel." If I don't cancel, I will receive 6 brand-new novels every month and be billed just $5.24 each for the regular-print edition or $5.99 each for the larger-print edition in the U.S., or $5.74 each for the regular-print edition or $6.24 each for the larger-print edition in Canada. That's a savings of at least 13% off the cover price. It's quite a bargain! Shipping and handling is just 50¢ per book in the U.S. and $1.25 per book in Canada.* I understand that accepting the 2 free books and gifts places me under no obligation to buy anything. I can always return a shipment and cancel at any time. The free books and gifts are mine to keep no matter what I decide.

Choose one: ☐ **Love Inspired® Suspense**
Regular-Print
(153/353 IDN GNWN)

☐ **Love Inspired® Suspense**
Larger-Print
(107/307 IDN GNWN)

Name (please print)

Address   Apt. #

City   State/Province   Zip/Postal Code

Mail to the **Reader Service:**
IN U.S.A.: P.O. Box 1341, Buffalo, NY 14240-8531
IN CANADA: P.O. Box 603, Fort Erie, Ontario L2A 5X3

Want to try 2 free books from another series! Call 1-800-873-8635 or visit www.ReaderService.com.

LIS20

SPECIAL EXCERPT FROM

Love Inspired

SUSPENSE

*An NYPD officer's widow becomes the target of
her husband's killer. Can her husband's best friend
and his K-9 partner keep her safe and take the
murderer down once and for all?*

Read on for a sneak preview of
Sworn to Protect *by Shirlee McCoy,*
the exciting conclusion to the
True Blue K-9 Unit *series, available*
November 2019 from Love Inspired Suspense.

"Come in," Katie Jameson called, bracing herself for the meeting with Dr. Ritter.

The door swung open and a man in a white lab coat stepped in, holding her chart close to his face.

Only, he was not the doctor she was expecting.

Dr. Ritter was in his early sixties with salt-and-pepper hair and enough extra weight to fill out his lab coat. The doctor who was moving toward her had dark hair and a muscular build. His scuffed shoes and baggy lab coat made her wonder if he were a resident at the hospital where she would be giving birth.

"Good morning," she said. She had been meeting with Dr. Ritter since the beginning of the pregnancy. He understood her feelings about the birth. Talking about the fact that Jordan wouldn't be around for his daughter's birth, her childhood, her life always brought her close to the tears she despised.

"Morning," he mumbled.

"Is Dr. Ritter running late?" she asked, uneasiness joining the unsettled feeling in the pit of her stomach.

"He won't be able to make it," the man said, lowering the charts and grinning.

She went cold with terror.

She knew the hazel eyes, the lopsided grin, the high forehead. "Martin," she stammered.

"Sorry it took me so long to get to you, sweetheart. I had to watch from a distance until I was certain we could be alone."

"Watch?"

"They wanted to keep me in the hospital, but our love is too strong to be denied. I escaped for you. For us." He lifted a hand, and if she had not jerked back, his fingers would have brushed her cheek.

He scowled. "Have they brainwashed you? Have they turned you against me?"

"You did that yourself when you murdered my husband," she responded.

Don't miss
Sworn to Protect *by Shirlee McCoy,*
available November 2019 wherever
Love Inspired® Suspense books and ebooks are sold.

www.LoveInspired.com

LISEXP1019R